THE BROTHERS LIONHEART

While you are reading this story, you will notice that it sometimes mentions a book called *The Brothers Lionheart*, which is by the famous Swedish author Astrid Lindgren. You don't really need to know the story of the Lionheart brothers to understand this one, but here's some information about it, which you might like to check out as you go along.

The Brothers Lionheart starts with the tragic death of two boys, Jonatan Lion, 13, and his brother Karl, known as Skorpan, who is 10. They enter another world called Nangijala.

Nangijala is being taken over by an evil tyrant called Tengil, who wants to rule the land and enslave its people. Jonathan and Skorpan become involved in the battle against Tengil.

The evil Tengil has a fire-breathing dragon called Katla. If anyone comes into contact with Katla's fire they become paralysed and die. Katla's only enemy is Karma, a mythical sea serpent that no one has ever seen.

The brothers have many adventures, and Skorpan overcomes his fear of Katla and Tengil and discovers his bravery. But Jonathan has been burned by Katla's fire and is going to die. The story ends with the two boys leaping over a cliff towards more adventures in the next world, Nagilima.

THIN ICE

ABOUT THE AUTHOR

Mikael Engström was born in 1961 and grew up in a suburb of Stockholm, Sweden. In the mid-1980s he studied photography for two years and started writing seriously. Nowadays he earns his living as a freelance journalist and photographer.

ABOUT THE TRANSLATOR

Susan Beard has been translating for over twenty years and specialising in literature for the last five. She has an MA in Literary Translation from the University of East Anglia and lives in Brighton, Sussex in the UK.

THIN ICE

mikael engström

TRANSLATED BY SUSAN BEARD

Little Island

THIN ICE
Published 2011
by Little Island
128 Lower Baggot Street
Dublin 2
Ireland

www.littleisland.ie

First published as *Isdraken* by Rabén & Sjögren, Sweden, in 2007.
Published by agreement with Rabén & Sjögren Agency.

Copyright © Mikael Engström 2007
English translation copyright © Susan Beard 2011

The author has asserted his moral rights.

ISBN 978-1-908195-00-5

British Library Cataloguing Data. A CIP catalogue record for this book is available from the British Library.

Cover design by Pony and Trap

Inside design by Sinéad McKenna

Printed in the UK by CPI Cox and Wyman

Little Island received financial assistance from
The Arts Council (An Chomhairle Ealaíon), Dublin, Ireland.

Little Island acknowledges the financial assistance of Ireland Literature Exchange (translation fund), Dublin, Ireland.

www.irelandliterature.com
info@irelandliterature.com

Little Island acknowledges the financial assistance of The Swedish Arts Council towards the translation of this book.

10 9 8 7 6 5 4 3 2 1

THE SNAKE

Mik was brushing his teeth. He looked at himself in the bathroom mirror. It was cracked in two diagonally, and one half was pushed in slightly. Only a millimetre, perhaps, compared with the other side, but it was enough to divide his face into two uneven halves. His face wasn't joined up. His ears looked big but that wasn't the mirror's fault. His ears were big. But they were the only things that were big. He was the shortest in the class – maybe the shortest in his whole year at school.

'Are your ears the only things that are growing?' the school nurse had asked, loud enough for everyone to hear.

The whole class had been queuing up to be weighed and measured, and a doctor with cold hands felt the boys' testicles inside their pants.

'Are your ears the only things that are growing?'

Before that, nobody had taken any notice of his ears, but afterwards they called him Bat Ears. Andreas had come up with that one. And on a scale of one to ten, how cool is Bat Ears?

Ploppy had only one testicle. It made him kind of famous,

in an odd sort of way. And Stefan, who always turned blue in gym, had something wrong with his heart – a hole between the compartments so the blood just sloshed backwards and forwards inside. He would never have to do gym again. And as for Sara, her breasts had grown massive overnight.

'Are your breasts the only things that are growing?' the school nurse hadn't said. They only said that about ears.

Ploppy's willy had also got big. Ridiculously big. No one said anything about that either. And Andreas had got hair. Everyone else in the class was totally healthy.

Mik got his mobile out. The display was cracked and the battery had died long ago, but that didn't matter. He wasn't connected to a network anyway, and besides, he didn't have a SIM card. Who would know if he was really talking to someone or just pretending? Mik's number was private and he never lent his phone to anyone. He could phone Dracula. He could phone evil Lord Tengil from *The Brothers Lionheart*. He could phone God.

He could phone anyone he liked. Maybe he should ring in sick? School wasn't his thing. It wasn't homework that was the problem – he didn't do any. The problem was all the hours spent locked in. Their classroom was on the ground floor and the windows had been fitted with bars after the school computers had been stolen for the third time. It was a prison.

Mik spent most of the lessons drawing. Whether it was maths, geography or English, he drew. His teacher was worried, naturally.

At break time you could have a game of hockey or play on the hill above the disused railway tunnel. You weren't really supposed to because a group of homeless winos lived down there in a camp made of tents and tarpaulins. The trains went through the new tunnels on the other side of the industrial estate. The entrance to the old tunnel was blocked off with a steel door and the rails had been broken up. It was a no man's land, tucked away out of sight. Parents and the school governors had tried to get the camp removed. The police had been there several times and pulled it down but the rough sleepers had soon built it up again.

There was a fat old woman wino too, with no bottom teeth. She used to squat down and pee in front of everyone.

At break, the boys stood on the hill above the tunnel entrance, looking down at the camp. There was no sign of any winos. It looked like a rubbish tip. Filthy clothes drying on the rusty fence. Cans and saucepans in the branches. Boxes and newspapers. Rotten old tents, green tarpaulins bleached by the sun and a few old bikes.

'Hello!' shouted Mik.

'Winos!' shouted Andreas.

Ploppy and Stefan looked around for ammunition and made a pile of stones, sharp from the tunnel blasting and ideal for throwing. Nothing happened. A tarpaulin flapped in a gust of wind. Bits of polystyrene blew about. An empty beer can rolled towards a car battery and stopped.

'Probably asleep,' said Ploppy.

'What? It's the middle of the day,' said Stefan.

'They can't stand the sunshine,' said Mik. 'They don't belong to this world.' He picked up a stone and yelled, 'Disgusting old cavemen!'

He threw the stone and it hit a tent.

Nothing happened.

Then everyone joined in. Andreas hurled a big rock, using a shot-putting technique. Stefan made himself go blue. It was raining stones.

The tent collapsed.

'What the hell? Stop!'

The stones whistled through the air and the people below crawled out of their homes, grimy, shaggy and haggard. To Mik they were evil beings, not people. Zombies from his nightmares, writhing, rotten.

Now they staggered out and were met by the sun. They were holding their arms over their heads and trying to get out of range. Tent after tent collapsed and a tarpaulin was ripped to shreds. Stones from the sky.

'I hate winos!' yelled Mik, and carried on throwing.

'Little sods!' they shouted back, trying to find shelter.

The old woman hauled herself out from under a tarpaulin and crouched down to pee, ignoring the stones bouncing all around her.

'Scumbag winos!' yelled Mik. 'Di-i-i-e!'

He threw and threw and threw, as hard and as fast as he could. Totally lost it. He picked up a large, sharp stone, but Ploppy pulled his hand down.

'That's enough now. Let's get out of here. It's stupid. Andreas and Stefan have legged it.'

Mik tried to throw his stone, but Ploppy stopped him.

'I've had enough. I'm off.'

'Di-i-i-ie!' shouted Mik. 'Drink yourselves to death, why don't you? Drink meths!'

Someone crawled out of a tent, a rumpled man in a filthy baby-blue padded jacket. Mik sent his stone flying, keeping his hand outstretched as if he were steering his missile towards its target. The stone whistled through the air in a perfect arc. The man down below turned round. Their eyes met – yellow, sick eyes.

Thump. He got him smack in the middle of the forehead. The man fell and didn't get up.

'Oops,' said Mik. And ran.

The teacher was setting up an archaic projector in the classroom.

'We're going to look at some pictures of old Hagalund,' she said. 'To see what it looked like before everything was knocked down and the blue tower blocks were built. We're going to have a history lesson about your own area. The place where you live. It's very interesting.'

Andreas put up his hand. 'Can't we look it up on the internet instead, Miss?'

'No, because we haven't got the new computers yet, after the last break-in. It will be three weeks before we get the new ones.'

Åsa's mobile started ringing. The teacher lifted her hand, pointing every finger at the class.

'Right. I'm telling you for the last time. All phones must be switched off or you'll have to hand them in every morning when you get here. I'll have to talk to the principal about this. We can never have a single lesson without –'

The classroom door burst open and the principal came rushing in. Everyone stared in astonishment and the teacher forgot what she was saying.

'Oh, we were just …'

The principal was a fat man in a blue shirt and tie. His shirt had dark patches of sweat under the arms and his face was redder than usual. He stared at the class, looking completely demented.

'I am absolutely furious,' he said. 'I've seen a lot at this school but this takes some beating …'

All the pupils looked at one another, not understanding a thing. Had he heard Åsa's mobile or what? Been standing outside with his ear pressed to the door? Unlikely.

The principal stepped out of the classroom and came back in again with a man in a baby-blue padded jacket that was striped with blood down the front. He was pressing a towel to his forehead. The towel had blood on it too.

The principal turned to the teacher. 'Your class was the only one to have break between twenty past nine and twenty to ten, and that's when this happened.'

Rigid with fear, Mik stared at the man. Him, here? How could he get into this world? Yellow eyes, big and black in the centre. He and Mik looked at each other. There was a rushing sound in Mik's head.

The rumpled, bearded old man held the towel to his forehead and slowly lifted his right arm to point at Mik. 'He threw the stone.'

Mik had to stay behind after school. He sat at his desk and his teacher pulled up a chair and sat down opposite him.

'The others threw stones as well,' said Mik, looking down. He was scribbling on the desk.

'Don't scribble on the desk.'

Mik carried on scribbling and said, 'It was only a wino, Miss.'

'*Only* a wino? How can you say that? Look at me, Mik. How are you feeling?'

'Good,' he said, still staring at the desk.

'I mean, really. How are things at home?'

'Good.'

The teacher stood up and walked over to Mik's box where he kept his drawings. She flicked through a thick pile of them. Lots of blood, ligaments, arms, legs, heads. And one or two eyes that had popped out.

'You draw only dismembered body parts. They are very well done – you're good at art. But what you draw … it's so … sick. There are hundreds of them. Is there nothing else you want to draw?'

Mik shrugged his shoulders and tried to smile. But he said nothing. His teacher picked up the bundle of drawings and sat down by him again.

'This picture – what's it supposed to be?'

She held up a piece of blood-red artwork. Flesh, ligaments and bones.

'It's a chopped-off hand, Miss.'

'Yes, I can see that. But why?'

'The colours are nice.'

Mik and his teacher sat in silence. She leaned closer to see what he had drawn on the desk. A long, rambling squiggle in pencil. Lines and circles tangled together in a very intricate pattern. There were no loose ends. Everything looped in endless trails.

'What is this supposed to be? Is it a snake?'

'I don't know,' said Mik. 'Thoughts, maybe.'

'You'll have to rub it out before you go. Then we'll see how we can sort this out.'

Mik rubbed and rubbed at the drawing on the desk. It all turned into a black mess. He had no idea what had to be 'sorted out'.

'Your dad didn't come to parents' evening.'

'He had a cold, Miss.'

On his way home from school, Mik stopped in the middle of the bridge and looked down at the blue commuter trains making sparks on the rails. The trains slowed down and came to a halt at Solna Station. People barged their way out of the doors and jostled along the platform to get to the bus first. To get home before ... yes, well.

Mik was in absolutely no rush to get home. He wanted Tony to be home first. It felt better that way.

He walked slowly along the pavement on Råsunda Road. A huge lorry thundered by, making the ground vibrate. A police car came driving past with its blue lights flashing and siren wailing. He hung around for a while outside the pizzeria, breathing in the aroma.

There was a tobacconist's on the corner. Its window was brown from all the traffic on Råsunda Road. Mik cleared a little peephole with his hand and there inside lay pipes in a row and open cigarette cases on a sun-bleached bed of green velvet. To the front of the window were shiny cigarette lighters in silver and gold. An open box was filled with dust-covered chocolates. And right in the middle of the window was a small stuffed crocodile leaking sawdust from a burst seam.

What was *that* doing there? And where had it come from? Africa? Or South America? Madagascar maybe? Perhaps it was a Nile crocodile.

Mik opened the door and went inside to ask. There were four steps down and a heavy smell of tobacco. It was nice – rich and musty. Cigar boxes and cartons of cigarettes were piled on shelves behind the counter. Gift-wrapped boxes of chocolates lay in compartments high up around the ceiling. Pipes and tins of tobacco were crammed together on the counter.

A tall, pale woman with jet-black hair came out through a dark red curtain behind the counter. Her eyes were incredibly green, like two gleaming jewels. She looked at him and lit a cigarette.

'Can you swim?' she asked, blowing smoke at him.

Mik hesitated. It was such an odd question.

'Children drown so easily. Can you swim?'

'Yes.'

She reached up high among the shelves, brought down two bars of chocolate and gave them to him. The bars were an odd shape. The chocolate had melted and set solid again.

'Can't be sold anyway. The box was left somewhere hot for while, but there's nothing wrong with the taste.'

'Thanks.'

Mik climbed the four steps up to the door, opened it and went out. The chocolate was the dark kind. He stuffed one of the bars into his pocket and pulled the silver paper off the other one. The squares were misshapen and covered with patches of white powder. He didn't like dark chocolate but he ate it anyway. It was free.

THE PIRATE

Tony was already home, sitting in his room in front of a computer with the name of the school branded into the plastic case. He was studying car mechanics and was way older than Mik. He would be seventeen next birthday. His room was a mess of dirty clothes and motorbike parts.

'Is Dad home?'

'No. You hungry? Shall I get dinner?'

'What have we got?'

'Sausages,' said Tony, closing down the sites he was looking at. 'Sausages and macaroni.'

'What's that?' asked Mik, pointing to a heap of flat boxes in the middle of the floor.

'DVD players with hard disk drives,' Tony answered with a smile. 'Came across them cheap. I've put one in your room. It's already connected to the TV. You can borrow some of my new films.'

'Horror?'

'Yeah, two zombie films. You'll like them.'

Tony was all right. Tony was everything a big brother should be. He had long blond hair, blue eyes and a smile that was secret and only for Mik. A smile to come home to when the world outside was crap. Tony smiled and everything was okay, as if he knew something no one else knew.

Mik was sure that Tony knew everything. Tony cooked the food, Tony looked after the money, Tony paid the bills. Without him everything would fall apart.

The hall was long and narrow, front door at one end, bathroom door at the other. Tony set the egg timer for ten minutes and put on a pair of blue hockey gloves. Mik put on his red ones.

'No punches in the face,' said Mik.

'No, not in the face. Not deliberately, anyway. Shoulders and stomach.'

The hockey gloves protected his hands. That was good. You dared to hit harder. Dared to hit as hard as you could, but a punch still felt just as painful as one with bare knuckles.

They faced each other in the middle of the hall, under the lampshade. Jogged a little on the spot, shook their arms and slapped their gloves together.

'Now,' said Tony.

The contest started, and Tony threw a fast punch straight at Mik's chest. It hurt. The next blow hit his shoulder. The first hits were the nastiest. After that, the places where he was hit lost all feeling.

Mik often went the whole round. Only a blow to the solar plexus could floor him. Or a forbidden punch on the nose.

After only a few seconds, Mik was pushed up against the bathroom door. He took blow after blow, but tried to break free with a series of wild punches. Tony danced backwards, laughing. He was out of Mik's reach. Tony was a head taller and had significantly longer arms. Mik flailed his arms and all Tony had to do was hold out his gloves and throw a few heavy punches. Mik warded him off with his hands, backed away. He was trapped again against the bathroom door, taking blow after blow.

'I give in.'

'Bell hasn't rung. Go the distance.'

'No.'

'Come on!' shouted Tony. 'Box.'

He skipped backwards, shaking his arms, giving Mik the chance to hit back.

'Don't curl up like a wimp. Fight, for God's sake.'

The inside of Mik's head seemed to turn red. He rushed forward, thrashing out wildly.

'Good,' shouted Tony. 'Come on!'

But Mik's punches didn't reach their target. He lunged until he was red and dripping with sweat, and started kicking. Tony took a wrestling hold on his little brother who wriggled and wailed and tried to get free.

'I'll stop now,' said Tony. He held Mik in a stranglehold until he calmed down. 'You mustn't get angry. Not angry, not annoyed. It's important not to take it personally. Take it personally and you're in trouble. We'll start again.'

They boxed until their bodies glowed with heat. The temperature in the hall rose. The sweat ran. Mik took a beating but he stood up, pressed against the bathroom

13

door, and there he stayed for the entire contest. Not once had he managed to drive Tony back towards the front door at the other end of the hall. Mik took the blows, thud, thud, thud.

The egg timer rattled. It was over.

Tony's fringe hung damply over his forehead. He smiled and ruffled Mik's hair with his hockey glove.

'You're getting better and better.'

Mik looked up at him, not letting his expression show how his body throbbed and stung.

'I went the whole round.'

There was a ring at the door. Tony looked through the peephole and held up his hand for Mik to be quiet.

It rang again, and then a third time. Time dragged. They stood silently, not moving. There was a fourth ring, then footsteps could be heard moving away down the stairs. Tony turned to face Mik.

'Don't ever open the door to anyone you don't recognise. If you're home on your own and see strangers out there, you mustn't open the door.'

'I promise.'

Mik tried out his DVD player, putting in a film. He could hear Tony washing up in the kitchen. It was comforting to hear the clatter of dishes. We're doing all right here, he thought. We're brothers and we're doing all right.

The Snake wasn't moving now.

Mik felt his shoulders. They were sore. It was a good

feeling afterwards, like now. A proud feeling. Bruises from a big brother.

The phone rang. Mik paused the film and the picture froze just as a zombie head exploded. He was about to answer when Tony came out from the kitchen and stopped him.

The brothers looked at each other. They knew what the call was about. After the fourth ring Tony picked up the handset.

'Hello.'

He listened for a moment.

'Yeah, we're on our way.'

Tony hung up and looked at the phone. It was frothy with washing-up liquid. The bubbles popped, one by one.

'We've got to go to The Pirate.'

The wind blew bitingly cold along Söderlång Street. Above the entrance a sign hung from rusty chains. The Pirate. Below the writing were two crossed swords. Tony opened the door and Mik followed him in. People inside were sitting eating or waiting for their food to be served. The waiting staff hurried between the tables. They were dressed in striped tops and aprons. From the ceiling hung sails and tankards. There was a smell of food and beer.

A waitress came towards them. Her striped top swelled over her breasts. She held her head tilted slightly to one side and was drying her hands on her apron.

'He's sitting down there. You'll find him, no problem. The usual place.'

15

Tony and Mik said nothing.

'He started causing trouble. The boss wanted to call the police, but it's calmed down now.'

She shrugged her shoulders and walked off to serve the customers.

The staircase down was narrow and wound between walls of thick uneven blocks of stone. It was like going down into a deep well. On a shelf at a turning were three skulls. The first was wearing a pirate's hat, the second was split open by a sword and the third had a patch over one eye and two teeth missing from its upper jaw. Someone had shoved a tab from a beer can into the gap.

'Are they real?' asked Mik.

'No, only plastic,' said Tony.

Mik stopped and looked at them.

'They look real to me.'

'Shut up. Don't worry about them. Come on.'

The bottom of the staircase opened into a large stone cellar. Drunken men and women with hoarse voices sat at solid tables. From the ceiling hung a pirate ship, sailing above the mad shrieking and the crazy laughter. Beer glasses spilled and it seemed to Mik that the people down here never left the place. Never saw the light of day. They sat here yelling, day and night. Condemned by some pirate king. And a steady stream of waitresses carried in frothing beer glasses and carried out empty ones.

Tony made his way between the tables, on the lookout. Mik followed close behind.

Someone stood up and bellowed to everyone to shut up, but the racket didn't stop.

'You bloody amateurs. Shut your faces.'

The person who was shouting stood there swaying and waving his arms up and down.

'Damned amateurs, the lot of you. Go to hell.'

And then he fell across the table and lay there.

It was their dad.

Tony shook him awake.

'Time to go home.'

THE SWIMMING TEST

Mik sat in a green vinyl chair that made his backside damp.

The school psychologist was called Lisa Nordahl. She had straight brown hair and kind brown eyes. Her voice was calm and beautiful but she asked weird questions.

Sitting in the green vinyl chair was like nothing else Mik had experienced. It was like being beamed up to another dimension. It was UFO time. The computer hummed and the screensaver jumped around. The room smelled strongly of cleaning fluid.

They had talked about his drawings. She said they reflected feelings that were somehow trapped. That they ought to try and get hold of them.

'What?'

'The feelings. Fear, perhaps. Loss, anger.'

'But they're only scary pictures,' said Mik. 'I like horror films and horror books and …'

Lisa Nordahl gave him a smile and leafed through her papers. Mik smiled back and fiddled with his mobile.

'Is it switched off?'

'Yes.'

'How do you feel about school?'

'Good.'

Lisa Nordahl managed to get her papers about Mik in order.

'You'll see that we're going to get to know each other really well.' Lisa Nordahl tucked a strand of hair behind her ear. 'What's it like for you at home?'

'All right.'

'That's good. I do wonder about that, though. Your dad hasn't been to any of the parents' evenings or progress assessments. He has …'

'Lots to do,' said Mik.

'Remind me what he does.'

'Lorry-driver.'

'That would keep him busy, then.'

'Yes.'

Lisa Nordahl's eyes wandered round the room. She moved a pen about and accidentally nudged the mouse, making the screensaver disappear. Her desktop background showed some little children playing with a hose on a green lawn.

'Tell me more about your dad.'

Mik looked out of the window. It was break and some pupils were playing hockey. Ploppy was goalie. Andreas was shouting something at him, hitting the goal with his stick. Mik realised he did not know his dad. When he thought of his dad he might just as well be thinking of a … spade.

Think spade.

Think spade.

19

Think spade.

Mik shrugged. Spade. What should he say to her? That he's always either drunk or hungover or both? That he doesn't hit him, but he cries a lot? That he's promised not to drink just as often as he's been drunk – they cancel each other out. Promise to be sober; be drunk. His dad could say, 'It's over now, I can't do this any more, I've finished drinking.' He had drunk so much he couldn't manage to do it any more. He was so tired of it that he … drank.

Clinking plastic bags. Bottles, everywhere bottles. Open bottles, empty bottles, broken bottles, hidden bottles. Mocking grins and bottles. Shouting and bottles. Crying and bottles. And then there were the bottles in the cellar. The days are too long, his dad said. The days are too long. The bottles made them shorter.

What rubbish words: bottles. Spottles. Spittles. Spit. Spew. Spade.

Tony hated Dad. 'I'll kill the bastard,' he always said.

Mik didn't say that. He felt no hate. You can't hate a spade. He only felt Snake Alone with his back-to-front scales, and when it started moving inside his body, it hurt. As long as he kept thinking 'Spade, spade' it kept still.

Think spade.

The computer hummed. The screensaver had started up again. Mik moved his bottom on the green plastic. It had stuck.

'Shall we think of a nice memory instead?' said Lisa Nordahl.

'Could do,' said Mik.

'Something to hold on to. An important memory which is, well, important. That makes you feel strong. Do you understand what I mean? If you say something good and keep that clearly in your mind it will be easier to talk about difficult things later on. Things that hurt. Things that are not nice and make you feel sad. We'll start with something really good. Do you understand?'

It went quiet. Lisa Nordahl's elbows were resting on the table, her head resting in her hands. She put her head on one side and raised her eyebrows.

'Hmm,' said Mik. 'Something good.'

He thought. Looked around the room. Lifted one buttock.

'One morning I walked down Dal Road to Råsta Lake. It was light, even though it was early. It was probably spring or nearly summer. Might have been about four a.m. I walked in the middle of the road. There were no cars, no people. I could pee on Råsunda Road. And over behind Vinter Road, on that big playing pitch, a fairground had sprung up overnight. It was so weird, totally unreal. I had found a fairground. It was just there. I've found lots of things – bikes, a camera, a broken guitar. But never a fairground.'

'What fun,' said Lisa Nordahl. 'Go on.'

'I ran home to tell Mum what I'd found. That it was amazing, a whole fairground. She said we could go there. That I could go on everything. We went there later that day. I was scared the fair would be gone, not be there any more.

But it was there. We went on the waltzer and the big wheel. The octopus was scariest. I had candy-floss and did the tombola and won a big green dog. But on the way home she got a pain in her chest, and the hill up Dal Road was too long for her. We sat on a fence and rested. But she laughed anyway because it had been so much fun at the fair.'

'That was beautifully told,' said Lisa Nordahl. 'That was lovely.'

Mik looked out through the window at his mates, who were playing hockey.

'I think that was the last time she laughed. It was probably the last time she went out.'

The school psychologist, Lisa Nordahl, made a move to write something down, but then she didn't write anything after all. The strand of hair had slipped out and she tucked it back behind her ear again. She had to put it behind her ear several times before it stayed there.

'Can I go now?'

'What?'

'We're doing swimming and I've got to get there in time.'

Solna Swimming Centre was a long walk from school. Ploppy had waited for Mik. They were going to be late.

'At least you missed English,' said Ploppy.

'Yeah, but I've got a damp backside,' said Mik.

'What did you talk about?'

'Nothing special.'

22

'You missed English to talk about nothing special?'

'She wanted to hear stories.'

'What about?'

'Anything.'

'Can we go back to yours today?' asked Ploppy.

Mik didn't know how to answer. Lately they had always been at Ploppy's. Ploppy's mum and dad were really nice. His mum made an incredible lasagne. Ploppy had got a super-fast PC which his dad had built, with the latest graphics card, crammed full of internal memory and with a massive hard drive. You could run the latest games with full high-resolution graphics.

'We're always at mine. Can't we go to yours?'

'No, impossible.'

'What, has your dad got a cold again?'

'No, we just can't. We're having visitors.'

They reached Vasalund and looked in the pet-shop window. A rabbit sat in a corner of its cage, frightened and trembling. Ploppy knocked on the glass. A couple of yellowy-green birds flapped around the minimal space inside a metal cage and damaged their feathers. A white rat scrabbled in the sawdust.

'Can you swim?' asked Mik.

'Obviously. Thousand metres, easily. You?'

'Sure, but maybe not a thousand metres. A couple of hundred or so.'

'That's enough,' said Ploppy.

'Did you know the world record for holding your breath under water is six minutes and three seconds? Peter Hirvell – he's German – he holds the record.'

The whole class had already changed and were at the deep end of the pool under the diving platform. Mik's swimming trunks were blue. He tensed his arm muscles and Ploppy laughed. As muscles go, they weren't up to much. Mik wasn't up to much, either. His skin was stretched over his ribcage, shoulders and hips as if his skeleton was covered in fine tissue paper.

The gym teacher, whose name was Ivan and who was known as Ive, stood in front of the class in a green tracksuit with a whistle round his neck and a stopwatch.

'Well,' he said, looking at his watch. 'Who would have thought it would be so flipping difficult to get here on time? I'll just have to repeat myself. We're doing a test today. A swimming test. You ought to be able to manage twenty-five metres. That's one length to pass the test. Line up by lane three here at the deep end.' And then he blew his whistle.

Andreas pushed his way to the front, leapt up onto the diving block, shook his arms and legs and warmed up with jumps and forward bends. Mik was shoved somewhere in the middle of the queue, behind Ploppy. The smell of chlorine made him feel sick and he thought of the German, Peter Hirvell.

Ive blew again on his whistle.

'Anyone who knows they can't swim is to get out of line now. I'm not planning on jumping in after you. As you can see, I haven't even changed.'

Ive stepped aside and studied them like an officer inspecting his troops.

'As I said, anyone who knows they can't swim one length can go to the heated baby pool for the time being.'

Someone giggled and they all looked over their shoulders, but no one left the line. Ive stopped alongside Mik, took hold of his shoulders with his huge, rough, ice-cold hands and turned him round once.

'What have you done? How did you get all these bruises?'

Mik looked up at him.

'Fell off my bike, sir.'

Up on the block, Andreas turned around. Impatient and flapping his body about.

'Sir, he hasn't got a bike. Can we start now?'

Ive made a worried face. Pulled a hair from his nose, blew the whistle and held up the stopwatch.

'You can dive or jump. I'll time you. Get going.'

Andreas dived, did the crawl for the entire length, heaved himself out of the pool and applauded himself as if he had won Olympic gold. Ive blew and the next person jumped in. Some swam the breast-stroke, others the crawl and one person used an unspecified method. Ive blew and called out the times. No one beat Andreas.

Ploppy chose a relaxed back-stroke, came off course and swam in a zigzag. His time was rubbish, but he got credit for a stylish technique. Just a little erratic.

Mik climbed up onto the block. Ive had his whistle in his mouth and was just about to blow it when Åsa started crying at the back of the line. Ive spat out the whistle and walked to the rear.

'Jump, then!' shouted Andreas.

'Get a move on; we're waiting,' said someone behind him. 'Hurry up.'

Åsa was still crying.

'Carry on at the front,' said Ive. 'I'll time you.' He blew his whistle.

Mik threw himself off the block.

'I think … I think my period's started,' said Åsa.

It was a quick journey down to the surface of the water, but an endless amount of time for thinking. Was he expecting a miracle? Or a world record? The choice had not been difficult. One person dies every time someone breathes. One in three people died in the plague.

He would miss Tony – that was the only thing he would miss. Well, Ploppy too, of course, but Tony most of all. The world's best big brother. It was a shame. Tough, but no hesitation. The choice between drowning or going to the heated baby pool was hard but not impossible. Perhaps all that stuff in The Brothers Lionheart about going to the land of Nangijala beyond the stars was true. But if it wasn't true, where would he end up instead?

Mik came up to the surface and then sank down into the depths. He was held gently, surrounded by bubbles and swirling water. There was no miracle. His arms and legs floundered, but he only sank deeper, drifting down to the bottom. The world record for holding your breath under water was six minutes and three seconds. Of course there were those who had been under longer, but they had hyperventilated or breathed in pure oxygen before they dived. That was cheating.

Six minutes and three seconds – would he beat that?

His eardrums ached. He remained lying on the tile floor of the pool, face upward. His hair waved slowly like thin seaweed and way up above he saw strange distorted shapes in a pale blue light. They bent over the edge and stared down. Swaying, ghostly beings.

But if he did manage six minutes and three seconds, who would know? He wouldn't even find out himself. If you drowned, your record was worthless.

The pressure increased in his chest, thudded throughout his whole body. His ears were filled with a powerful ringing. His heart pumped and pumped, faster, faster. His blood screamed for air; he was burning up and what he heard was singing. Someone was singing. A murmuring song. Where was that coming from? His field of vision shrank, the edges turned red and the song rose higher and higher. Notes without a tune. Rising, falling. Like crying. It was weird and it became weirder.

He saw his mum. Her face quivered behind the waves, had no real shape. She had a green umbrella.

Everything disappeared.

Mik woke by the edge of the pool, coughing up chlorinated water. His body hurt as if stuck by a thousand burning hot needles. His nose was stinging and the pressure in his chest made him feel he was being turned inside out. His heart pounded fast and hard.

Ive crouched over him. His clothes were wet and his hair dripped. His whistle and stopwatch dangled above Mik's face. The class stood in a silent circle around them. Mik vomited up the school canteen meat loaf. His classmates stepped back.

'How are you?' said Ive, stroking back his own wet hair. 'Do you feel okay?'

Mik nodded.

'Nobody told me you went under. I went with Åsa to the changing room. She was … ill. I didn't know anything until Ploppy came running to get me. They thought you were play-acting.'

Mik nodded again.

'Are you sure you're okay?'

'Yes, sir,' said Mik wearily. 'What was my time?'

'The watch has stopped on three zero five. It's not waterproof.'

'Three zero five!'

'Go to the small pool,' said Ive. 'You've done enough for today.'

Mik got up on wobbly legs and staggered off. Ive blew his whistle and the next pupil dived in. Mik slid down into the warm water of the baby pool.

Three zero five.

SNAKE ALONE

It seemed a long way home from Solna Swimming Centre. Mik walked slowly, his head aching. He felt sick and stopped when he came to the tobacconist's shop. The crocodile was lying there in the window, leaking sawdust. It was pitiful. Perhaps it had once swum in the waters of the Nile, hunted small fish and then, feeling full, crawled up onto a sandy beach to rest in the sun by some pharaoh's temple. And now here it was in a grimy shop window on Råsunda Road in Solna, leaking sawdust. It had probably never expected that.

The tobacco lady beckoned him in from the other side of the window. Mik opened the door and went the four steps down. His knees were giving way.

'You look ill,' she said. 'Do you feel all right?'

'We had a swimming lesson. It was hard.'

'I've got some more chocolate I can't sell; that would be tricking people. But there's nothing wrong with it at all; it just needs eating.'

She handed Mik some bars of chocolate.

'Thanks.'

'How's your dad?'

'Got a cold.'

'Oh.'

Her pale face smiled and her green eyes bored right through him. Green lasers. But what did she know about his dad?

'Nothing is predetermined,' she said. 'There's always a choice and you decide.'

'Me? No, I don't decide anything. I don't even know who does decide. Tengil, maybe.'

'You exist, therefore you decide.'

He thought for a while, but he did not feel as if he existed. Customers came into the shop.

'Go on then, take the chocolate and go.'

Mik waited a second or two. There was something he had meant to ask but he had forgotten what it was.

~~~

Mik put his key in the door, but it was already unlocked. It was quiet in the flat. He could make out the sour smell of red wine. Dad was lying on the kitchen floor. He had fallen off the chair and dragged the tablecloth and a bottle of wine with him. The wine had run out in a large red puddle. Mik shook him. Nothing happened. He was dribbling.

The front door slammed. Tony was home and came into the kitchen.

'Oh, shit.'

'Shall we help him into bed?' asked Mik. 'It's hard, lying on the floor.'

'You know what?' shouted Tony. 'As far as I'm concerned he can lie on a bed of nails.'

'But,' said Mik, 'it's –'

31

'He's finished. It's all finished. This isn't going to work.'

Tony walked up and down the kitchen. Took a swipe at the empty bottles standing on the draining board and knocked them over. Mik didn't know what to say. Tony grabbed hold of a bottle.

'I ought to smash this into his head.'

He waved the bottle in the air. Tried to break it against the sink but it stayed in one piece.

Mik fetched the hockey gloves and wound up the egg timer.

'Want to box?'

'You want to box, do you?'

'It's fun.'

Tony searched through the freezer and the kitchen cupboards.

'You want to box? He's lying here, drinking up all our money. We haven't got any food at home. Box? You must be mad.'

'I've got chocolate. Several bars. Want some?'

'Don't you get it, little Mik? He's a bloody drunk,' Tony yelled.

'We can play Monopoly. You can have Norrmalm Square.'

'I'm getting out of here,' said Tony. 'I'm going to sleep over at Dennis's.'

'What am I supposed to do, then?' said Mik. 'He can't lie here like this.'

'Forget him. Play a video game. Let him be. Watch a film or borrow my PC. I'm out of here.'

Tony left, slamming the door.

It was silent.

Watch TV.

Alone.

Alone in the flat.

Alone with Dad.

It was more lonely than when you actually were alone.

Watch TV.

Alone started to tear at his stomach.

Alone was a snake with skin that stung.

He writhed in your stomach, coiling around with sharp, back-to-front scales. Scales that scratched and scraped and tore. Think of something good; think of something fun. Think of something good, good, good. Important and good, Lisa Nordahl had said. Such as what?

Could he phone someone? Who? And what should he say? Could he phone Ploppy and ask if he could go round to his place?

Mik phoned Ploppy.

'Weren't you having people round?'

'They didn't come.'

'Well then, I can come to you,' said Ploppy.

'No.'

'Why not?'

'See you tomorrow.'

'Okay, see you tomorrow.'

Mik fetched a blanket and spread it over his dad. It looked

as if he had crash-landed. Fallen from a great height. His cheek was pressed flat against the floor. He needed a pillow. Mik went and got one of the small cushions from the sofa, lifted his dad's limp head by the hair, shoved the cushion underneath and let his head down again.

Think of something good and important. Make Snake Alone be still and go to sleep.

Mik sank down to the floor and leaned against the fridge. Some magnets fell and unpaid bills fluttered down. Slowly he unwrapped the last bar of chocolate. It was so quiet; there was only the tick of the egg timer and the faint hum of the fridge. He could make out the sound of the neighbour's television. They were dead sounds, lonely sounds. Someone flushed a toilet.

My dad, thought Mik, and looked up at the ceiling. My dad drives a lorry during the day and is saving up for a bike for me, with twenty-one gears. Or a computer faster than Ploppy's. With a graphics card so good the games look like real films. In the evenings we build models together. And we go fishing a lot. But only in the summer when it's lovely and warm. He's got a red reel on his fishing rod. Mine's silver. And I usually get to row the boat. That's how it was.

This evening they would probably carry on making the model of the German battleship Bismarck. Only the funnels were left and a few small details like the lifeboats. Tricky to get right.

Mik put the last piece of chocolate into his mouth. There was a ring at the door – the sound scared him to death. Ding dong right into his heart. Who was that, now?

And why?

Had Tony forgotten his keys?

The peephole revealed a woman and a man out on the staircase. Strangers. He must absolutely not open the door to people he didn't recognise. Tony had forbidden it. Strangers want strange things. The man was bald and had a gold front tooth. The woman had long blonde hair and a green mac. She took out a mobile and a second later the hall phone behind Mik rang. The man reached out his hand and rang the doorbell again. Mik held his breath. The woman rested her ear against the door to listen. Her earring was in the shape of a parrot. There was one more ring, then they left.

The egg timer rattled on the draining board in the kitchen. Mik ran into his room, threw himself onto his bed and pressed a pillow against each ear.

STRANGERS

The class stood outside the enormous entrance to the museum. Their teacher tried to gather them together, to get them in some kind of order. Andreas and Stefan ran round pushing the girls. Stefan's face turned blue. Ploppy balanced along the top of a wall.

'Stop!' yelled the teacher. 'And get down from that wall.'

Mik stood with his head tilted upwards, looking at the façade of the building. It was a very impressive building, like a castle, with towers at each end and a dome. A flock of birds settled on the dome. Were they jackdaws or crows? Last summer he had looked after an injured jackdaw until it was well enough to fly. It wasn't a good pet. It crapped everywhere.

Mik looked down again and found the class had disappeared. He opened the door and went in. The ceiling was high and there was no one about. Distant laughter and shouting and the clatter of heels echoed faintly from staircases and galleries. A warm, dry smell of age and mustiness filled his nostrils and right in front of him stood two four-legged skeletons. Enormous skulls with long curved tusks and empty black eye sockets. They were elephant skeletons; he could tell that from the tusks. To the left was a glass display case containing a stuffed tiger eating an animal it had hunted down. The tiger was dusty and faded. Not yellow and black but grey and black. On a small gold label on the plinth it said, 'Tiger with prey, 1927'.

Glass cases with dusty animals in them filled the entire gallery. An elephant calf, coming apart at the seams, had lost its tail. Astonished gorillas glared through the glass. Monkeys clung to branches. The largest case was made to look like a savannah scene with ostriches, two zebras, vultures and a giraffe. All the animals were unbelievably dead.

Mik noticed he was being followed by a man in a blue shirt and black trousers. A mystery man, as dry and wrinkled as the dusty animals. Mik walked through the rooms, saw strange-looking fish, peculiar birds, a panda, a hippopotamus, a gigantic tortoise and a crocodile that was way bigger than the tobacco lady's.

The man followed him stealthily, watching him through glass cases and over the top of cabinets.

There was a calf with two heads and an extinct Tasmanian tiger. Each animal had a small tombstone of gold which gave the name of the animal, where it came from and when it had died.

Mik went up to the next floor and through a heavy door. He came out onto a bridge stretching high above a large gallery. The air was cold and stale. Mik stood amazed and wide-eyed among colossal skeletons. Some hung from the ceiling on steel wires. The biggest ones were on the floor below. They were whales: a baleen whale, a blue whale, a sperm whale and an orca. Vertebrae as big as tree stumps were attached to other vertebrae with metal fixtures. Enormous heads followed by ribs which joined together as they reached the tails. In black felt-tip on the biggest skull someone had written 'shag'.

There was an open booth like a telephone kiosk in the middle of the bridge. Inside was a loudspeaker and a button that Mik pressed. The whale sound started up. Long-drawn-out, mournful sounds.

'They're singing,' said someone standing behind Mik.

It was the mystery man. On his shirt was a badge which said 'Security'. The whale sound came to an end with a scraping noise in the loudspeaker.

Mik stayed where he was in the booth, not making a sound. He looked at the museum guard and thought he was going to be told off for something. Anything at all: that he was there, that someone had written a rude word on the skeleton. Or because he had dared to press the button. Or because he existed.

'The whales come from Gondwana,' said the museum guard. 'A lost continent. Although that's hard to believe. Their ancestors lived on land, but that was a long time ago. Sixty million years.'

'On land?' said Mik.

'Yes. They're not fish, if that's what you thought. Whales are mammals with the largest lungs in the world. They were

38

four-legged animals, a kind of dog, before they stepped into the water and left all the land animals behind.'

'How do you know that?'

'If you look at a whale's penis there's no doubt it was once a dog.'

'Its penis?'

'Yes.'

The guard reached across in front of Mik and pressed the whale-song button again.

'Listen. They're singing to each other. They're keeping the herd together and singing in the depths of the ocean. They can be underwater for an hour before they have to come up for air. But sometimes they suffocate.'

'Drown?'

'Kind of. They swim the wrong way, up onto land. Whales haven't got a breastbone so they suffocate under their own weight on the shore. Whole herds can swim together onto dry land and die.'

'Why?'

'Nobody knows. But I think they lose their magnetic compass.'

The whale song ended.

Mik pressed the button again and said, 'Perhaps they are longing to be on land again.'

He turned around but the guard had gone.

His class rushed into the whale gallery. The boys bellowed and shrieked and the sounds echoed between the skeletons.

Stefan's face was blue. Åsa and her friends held their noses and made vomiting gestures at the smell. Their teacher's forehead was shiny with sweat.

'Look,' said Andreas. '"Shag".'

Ploppy and Stefan pushed Mik out of the booth and pressed the button until the sound got stuck and the whales just howled. Mik looked for the museum guard but couldn't see him anywhere.

~~~

Their teacher had managed to get the class onto the 509 bus to Solna. Mik and Ploppy sat next to each other. The bus set off. Their teacher stood in the aisle and held on and tried to control her pupils.

'You disappeared,' said Ploppy to Mik.

'No I didn't. You were the ones who disappeared.'

'We saw a stone from the moon. A little stone we got from America. They brought it home with them when they went to the moon.'

'I missed that.'

'It was just an ordinary stone.'

'Did you know the whale was once a dog?'

'No,' said Ploppy, pulling a stupid face. 'A whale has always been a whale.'

'Wrong. Sixty million years ago it was a dog.'

'Yeah, right,' said Ploppy, picking his nose. 'And Godzilla lives in Solna Swimming Centre.'

'You can tell from its penis,' said Mik.

The bus stayed at the same bus stop for a long time. A passenger who had got on was causing trouble with the driver.

'Whales can hold their breath for an hour,' said Mik.

But Ploppy didn't answer. He was looking along the aisle to the front of the bus.

Sara pointed and said, 'Look at that idiot.'

Mik craned his neck to see the front. A stocky, drunk man stood there, swaying and shouting at the driver, who answered calmly, 'You can't get on. That's all there is to it. I make the decisions here. Either you get off or I'm calling the police on my radio.'

'Listen, you baboon. You can go to hell, you and the rest of this bus. Here I am, a member of the public, and I'm not allowed to get on.'

Mik had stopped breathing. The pressure built up in his head. His blood pounded and his ears were burning bright red. An older man in front of Mik turned to the woman beside him and said, 'These winos. You get sick and tired of them. There seem to be more and more these days.'

A young man in a leather jacket shouted, 'Throw him off, let's go.'

'Get a move on,' called a few girls who were sitting right at the back.

The drunk man stepped off the bus, shouting and swearing. The doors closed, the bus driver pulled away. The whole class started talking quietly and whispering spread from seat to seat. Some giggled. Some laughed out loud.

'What's the matter with you?' asked the teacher, looking from pupil to pupil.

The laughter faded away. No one answered, but some grinned and opened their eyes wide and there was more whispering. The teacher shook her head and looked at them in surprise.

'What are you whispering about? It was only an old drunk.'

'It was Mik's dad,' said Stefan.

Mik had heard everything that was said and whispered. The words were being sucked round like screams inside his brain. Tumbling and bouncing against the walls of his skull, the words refused to stop and be put in order. It was as if someone had forced a hand blender into his head and switched on the sharp blades. His brain became red gloop. Round and round, until it screamed. And it was a thousand years to the next bus stop. Snake moved about inside him.

The bus stopped and the doors opened. Mik rushed off and the class pressed their noses to the windows.

For hours he wandered around aimlessly in the rain. It had started as snow but now it was raining. The neon lights of the shops were reflected in the wet asphalt, cold blue colours, cruel green colours and angry red colours.

Should he go home?

He didn't want to.

Should he go ...?

Where was there to go if not home?

Everyone goes home.

He stopped outside the tobacconist's, rubbed the dirty window with his mitten and looked at the crocodile. What a rotten life it had now it was dead, lying here leaking sawdust while the buses and cars thundered past.

Why is it in the shop window? That's what I was going to ask.

Mik went in. The tobacco lady sat on a chair behind the counter, smoking a cigarette in a long weird holder. She blew smoke up at the ceiling and said, 'Never start smoking. It's expensive and unhealthy.'

'Why is there a crocodile in the window?'

'Why?' She looked surprised. 'Why? I don't know.'

'You don't know?'

'No. Do I have to? Does a person have to know everything?'

Mik couldn't find anything to say. She gave him a couple of bars of chocolate and he left.

Mik waited inside the entrance for Tony, waited for him to come on the bus from school. The light had gone out. He didn't press the timer button, which was glowing red, but stood inside in the dark, looking through the glass doors. Ate the chocolate and watched the bus stop. He was cold in his wet clothes, tried to warm himself against the radiator, thinking: if you have a crocodile in your window, you ought to know why.

Buses came and people hurried off to get home quickly. Mik took out his mobile and wondered who he should ring. The principal, perhaps. Tell him he'd left school for good. Or ring the man in the baby-blue jacket. Say he was sorry. Tell him he hadn't meant it. Or had he? Had he meant to do it? If you throw a big, sharp stone at someone you ought to know why. Did he know? Mik considered it for a while, staring out at the bus stop. He was chilled right through to his backbone; he pressed himself harder against the radiator. Played with the buttons on the mobile, put it to his ear.

'Hello. Sorry.'

A police car pulled up at the pavement. Two police officers were sitting in the car. They put on the interior light and shuffled pieces of paper about, and one of them wrote something on a pad. The 515 bus pulled up on the other side of the street and a stream of people hurried off the bus towards the train station.

Tony came walking diagonally across the road. Mik was happy. His big brother. They would make dinner together, play video games. Do some boxing.

The policemen stepped out of the car and stopped Tony. They spoke for a little while and then led him to the car, opened the back door, pushed him inside and drove off. Mik ran out and watched the car disappear. Saw the red rear lights blend in with all the other red rear lights in the rush-hour traffic.

Why had they taken him with them? Mik didn't understand. He was shoved left and right by people hurrying through the rain to get home and couldn't understand any of it.

The door was unlocked. Dad was lying on the kitchen floor. On the table was an empty spirits bottle and a collection of beer cans. He was bleeding from a cut on his temple. He had hit himself on the window sill and dragged the plant pot and the curtains with him. Mik fetched a cushion and a blanket. Covered him over, lifted his head, pushed in the pillow. His dad opened his eyes. It was a blank look, as if no one existed behind them. There was only emptiness and darkness.

'Can you hear the music?' he said.

'No.'

'It's the cooker; it's playing music. Hear it?'

'Dad, there's no music. The cooker can't play music.'

Mik became frightened. He looked at the cooker but couldn't hear anything. His dad shivered with cold under the blanket.

Tony had to come. Tony would know what to do. They had to –

The doorbell rang. It's Tony. It must be Tony. He's forgotten his keys. It must be … he's …

Mik rushed to the door and opened it, and there outside stood the strangers. The woman with the parrot earrings and the man with the gold tooth.

'Hello. Are you Mik?'

He tried to shut the door, but Gold Tooth held onto the handle.

'We're from the social services. I'm called Linda and this is Kent,' said the woman with the parrot earrings.

Mik looked at them. What did they want?

'Is your dad home?'

'No,' said Mik. 'He's doing overtime.'

'But he's out of work.'

'No, he drives a lorry.'

'I see,' said Gold Tooth.

There was a crash from the kitchen. A chair fell over.

'I don't want to hear the music. Turn off the music. Please, help me. Turn off ...'

Parrot Earrings took a step into the hall.

'Is that your dad who –'

'He's got a cold,' said Mik.

The strangers went into the kitchen. His dad crawled across the floor for a short distance and then collapsed.

'You can't get a worse cold than this,' said Gold Tooth, and crouched down beside Mik's dad.

Then they took it in turns to talk to Mik.

'We're here to help you.'

'Your dad will also get help. He's very ill.'

They phoned for an ambulance.

'We can put you in a temporary home for tonight. Would you like that?'

'No,' said Mik. 'I live here.'

'Can you sleep here tonight?'

'I always sleep here every night.'

The man and the woman looked at each other.

'But you can come with us instead. It might be a bit … lonely here.'

'No, my big brother's coming soon, he's almost seventeen and …'

The ambulance came quickly. Two men in green with an orange stretcher. They got Mik's dad into a sitting position and spread a yellow blanket over him. 'Hospital Property', it said on the blanket.

'Are you sure you'll be able to manage tonight?'

'Yes. Tony's coming soon.'

'Where is he now?'

'He's probably … at football practice.'

Parrot Earrings wanted to take Mik with them there and then, but he refused and locked himself in his room. They slid a note under his door with a phone number so he could ring if he wanted anything. Mik listened through the door.

'Will you be all right, then? Is there any food in?'

'I've already eaten and Tony will be here soon.'

'Your family will get help. Everything will be all right. We'll soon get this sorted out.'

They left.

The flat became silent and empty. Mik switched on all the lights, even the ones in the toilet and the big hall cupboard. But the Snake had woken up. Mik put on both the radio and the TV.

The Snake began to move.

Tony would be angry. Strangers weren't to be allowed in, but that was exactly what he had done, and they had taken Dad to hospital.

He picked up a large cushion, lay in front of the TV and wondered if it was good or if it was bad. Something big had happened, one way or another, but what it was he didn't know. Who had he let in? And what would happen now?

He didn't want to watch any of Tony's horror films. He put an old tape in the video player: *The Brothers Lionheart*, which he must have seen a hundred times. He knew the story inside out. The tape was worn, the picture fuzzy, with flickering lines. Tengil's men stood up on the wall with swords and spears. Black helmets and flapping cloaks. And there were the brothers, Skorpan and Jonatan. Mik fell asleep in front of the television.

'Mik. Wake up.'

Tony was shaking him.

'Mik, where's the old man?'

'I let them in.'

'Who?'

'They took Dad.'

'Took Dad?'

'In an ambulance.'

Mik found the note he had been given and handed it to Tony.

'Solna Social Services,' said Tony.

'We're going to get help.'

PART 2

LAND OF ICE
⚡

THE JOURNEY

Mik put on his outdoor clothes and tied the laces of his trainers. He had already packed his bag early that morning. The woman with parrots in her ears lifted it into the boot of the car.

'Now, have you got everything?'

'Yes.'

'Haven't you got any better shoes?'

'No.'

'It's a small bag,' she said, trying to pretend to be his friend.

But she wasn't his friend. She was the woman with the parrots in her ears. Never, ever would he be her friend.

They climbed into the car.

'The bus leaves the city terminal at twenty past twelve. We'll have to hurry. Put your seat-belt on.'

They stopped and started all the way out of Solna, past Norrtull and into Stockholm. There was a lot of traffic and a lot of red traffic lights. As they waited for green she looked at him and chatted in an artificial voice, as if she was trying to be a child herself, but what she was saying was completely incomprehensible.

'Do you know what is going to happen now?'

'No. How would I know that?'

The traffic lights changed to green.

'Well, it's like this,' she said, accelerating away from the lights. 'Social services can offer parents and children support and help if they want it, according to the social services legislation. That's the law that tells us how to look after families with problems.'

'Oh,' said Mik, looking at all the buildings, signs and people.

Taxis sounded their horns. A lorry was stopped in the middle of the road as goods were being unloaded. A bus tried to get past with only millimetres to spare. It started to rain. Parrot Earrings switched on the windscreen wipers.

'Your dad will be in a treatment centre for six weeks and you are going to live with his sister, your aunt. It's going to be a long journey. You'll get there tomorrow. We couldn't make a better arrangement at such short notice.'

'I can live at home,' said Mik.

'Not on your own.'

'With Tony. He's my big brother.'

'Tony won't be living at home either.'

'Is he coming to auntie's, then?'

'No.'

'Why not?'

'We're nearly there now. We've just got to find your bus.'

'Can I come home again?'

'Of course. This is only a temporary solution. Everything's going to be fine. That's my job, you could say.'

'What? Making things fine?'

She smiled at him. He did not smile back at her. No one had asked him anything. It had all just happened. He was given money and he bought his ticket himself from the bus driver. The bus was going to Umeå and from there he had to get a bus to the end of the world. Parrot Earrings had written it all down on a piece of paper.

Mik chose a seat by the window, the bus pulled away and she waved from outside. He did not wave back.

He hadn't met Auntie Lena for several years. At the funeral, maybe. Dark hair, big brown eyes and a husky voice. That was all he could remember about her. And that she lived way up in northern Sweden, so far away that they had never been to visit her. He had no idea whether she was nice or nasty or hard work.

There was a TV on the bus, showing a film he couldn't understand. Mik leaned his head against the cool glass. The bus swayed gently. The evening rushed past outside a rainy window. Grey and dreary. Someone's mobile rang; there was low chatting and the rustling of a crisp packet.

Mik woke with his forehead against the glass and a stiff neck. It was dawn and the whole landscape was white. The snow lay thick and it weighed down the branches of the fir trees. There was forest, forest and more forest. The wilderness seemed endless but every so often a house appeared or a whole farm. Then the buildings grew gradually closer. They drove into a large town and there he changed to another bus. The driver helped him find the right one.

Mik was on the coast and would now be travelling many kilometres inland. The second bus was old and rattled and smelled horrible. There were only a few passengers.

Forest, forest, forest.

After a two-hour drive along bumpy roads, houses began to appear among the trees. No big buildings, no blocks of flats, but small, pretty houses with hats of snow. The mounds left by the snow ploughs were enormous and the snow was incredibly white. Never had he seen so much winter. 'Centre', it said on a sign.

The bus swung into a little square and pulled up between two grocery stores, Konsum and ICA.

Was this the shopping centre?

A few people were standing in the square, waiting by their steaming cars. Not many people got off the bus: Mik, two ladies and a young man in a military uniform with a huge rucksack.

It was cold, terribly cold. The snow creaked under his shoes. Mik looked around the square, but there was no one there who could be his aunt. The driver opened the luggage compartment and Mik was handed his bag. The ladies and the soldier were hugged by the people who had come to meet them. They laughed and said, 'Oh, it's been so long since we saw you.'

'How was the journey?'

'Was there snow in Stockholm?'

'Anything happen in the village?'

'What could possibly happen here?'

The people meeting the passengers packed their luggage into the cars and drove off. The bus drove off too. Mik stood all alone in a snow-covered square in a snow-covered village. He looked at the green Konsum sign then turned his head in the other direction and saw the red ICA sign.

The minutes lengthened into a quarter of an hour. The cold made its way through the soles of his shoes and up into his feet. His knees began to shake. The cold travelled further up into his stomach and met the cold coming down through his head. His whole body shook.

An old man came along on a kick sledge. He had fish in a box on the seat.

'What are you waiting for?' said the old man, who had a fat red nose and bushy eyebrows that met in the middle.

'My auntie.'

'Auntie?' said the old man and looked around the empty square. 'Did you come on the bus?'

'Yes.'

'Then perhaps you came on the wrong day.'

The old man parked his sledge outside the Konsum shop, picked up the box of fish and went in.

Wrong day, thought Mik. I can't have come on the wrong day. I came today. When else would I have come? I don't even know where I've come to. I don't know anything.

He tramped up and down on the spot to get warm. The man came out with an empty box, put it in the sledge and set off.

A few children the same age as Mik came running across the square, their toboggans bouncing behind them. They came to a standstill, staring at him. There were two boys and a girl and they were better dressed for winter than Mik, with their thermal trousers, padded jackets and woolly hats. They stood there and stared for a while. Mik held his bag in his hand and stared back. It started to snow.

'Look what big ears he's got,' one of the boys said. He had snot running from his nose.

'And red,' said the other one.

'He's freezing,' said the girl, who had long dark hair and a large blue-black birth mark under her right eye.

'Who is it?'

'Probably came on the bus.'

'What for?'

Mik couldn't stop himself staring at the birthmark. It looked like a third eye.

'What are you staring at? The birthmark? I'm having an operation to take it away.'

'Oh,' said Mik.

'Know what?' said the boy with the runny nose. 'You ought to have an operation to get rid of your ears.'

Laughing, they ran into Konsum, coming out a moment later with bulging bags of sweets. Only the girl turned round and looked at him with her three eyes. She pulled her earlobe and smiled. Mik took out his mobile and pretended to answer an important phone call.

The snow fell even more heavily. One or two people went into ICA to do some shopping, and one or two people went into Konsum. But not many. For long periods of time he stood completely alone in the square.

Somewhere far off a dog barked. A car skidded at the road junction. Snow settled on his head and shoulders. He was so cold his teeth chattered. His feet ached.

It was already starting to get dark. It was strange – it had only just got light and now it was getting dark again. He had come to a place with very short days. He had come to the wrong place. He didn't want to be here.

The old man with the kick sledge came back with a new box of pike on the seat. He stopped in front of Mik.

'And what are you waiting for?'

'I told you, my auntie.'

'Auntie?'

'You've already asked me that,' said Mik.

'What? Did I ask you?'

'Yes. A little while ago.'

'You're getting snowed on.'

The old man parked his sledge outside the ICA store and went in with his box of fish. Mik watched him. He must have a short memory, but that's probably what happened here. Their memories froze solid.

How long would he be standing here waiting? He could have walked to Lena's house if only he knew where she lived. Soon his own memory would freeze solid.

The old man came out again with an empty box.

'Cosmos,' he said. 'The cosmos is only an idea. Think about that.'

'What?' said Mik, his teeth chattering.

The old man lifted his sledge and turned it round.

'Synchronicity.'

'Synchro what?'

'You've got snow on your head.'

And off he went.

Mik moved his legs up and down. He couldn't work it out. His feet started to go numb. He couldn't stand here any longer. He would freeze to the spot and be left there like a big-eared snowman. And no doubt one strange person after another would come up to him and say strange things.

Mik went into Konsum and stood in the warm air between the inner and outer doors.

The woman at the till and a few customers looked at him. He pretended not to see and fixed his eyes on a notice board.

Someone was selling a pram. Someone else wanted winter tyres for a Saab. A man called Tore was hoping to find his cat, a black one with a white patch on its neck and one white front paw. There was no mention of a reward, so Mik thought that was probably the last Tore had seen of his cat. Bea Svensson's cat was also missing. It was a farm cat, a tabby. The reward was fifty kronor. Someone called Lisa Erikson was asking for information about her tortoiseshell female cat that had been missing since October. The reward for Lisa's cat had also been fifty kronor but that had been crossed out and increased to a hundred.

Mik read on and was surprised, because among the notices about sledges, freezers, lingonberries, fishing reels and tyres there were at least ten about missing cats. Some with rewards, some without. It was odd. He looked out through the glass doors. Somewhere out there in the forest must be a whole herd of lost cats.

Mik went through the inner automatic doors, stood in front of the till and asked, 'When is the next bus home?'

The cashier smiled at him.

'Home?' she said.

'Yes, home.'

'You mean the next bus to leave here?'

'Yes.'

'Thursday.'

THE HAWK OWL

A dirty old Volvo estate rolled into the square. Out of the car stepped a woman in a green anorak. She had large eyes and long dark hair. People who guessed her age usually put it at just under thirty, but she was actually forty-two. The woman looked around the empty square, bewildered. Customers inside Konsum stared out through the window.

A woman who stood by the checkout paying for her items snorted, 'Oh, her. She's crazy.'

The woman leaned over towards the checkout lady and whispered very loudly, 'She's one of those lezzies.'

The cashier handed over the change and said, 'She can be whatever she likes, as long as she does her shopping here at Konsum. And that's only a rumour. Spiteful gossip.'

The woman took her change and very carefully put it into her purse.

'I think she should do her shopping at ICA. Everyone knows what's going on. Why would an attractive woman like her be living on her own?'

'We don't have any prejudice here,' said the Konsum checkout lady.

'And she calls herself a district nurse,' said the woman, packing her shopping. 'Imagine someone like that being allowed to have that kind of job. And why hasn't she got any children?'

Mik picked up his bag and walked out into the square. He had recognised her. It was Lena, his dad's sister. She saw him and came rushing up.

'There you are. Sorry, I had to see to Gustavsson. He's a right old moaner and refuses to go to the health centre even though his toes have turned blue.'

She crouched down and gave him a big hug. Mik stiffened. Something strange was happening inside his body. His joints locked. Lena noticed it immediately.

'It's a long time since anyone held you, isn't it?'

She pushed Mik away from her, holding onto his shoulders, and looked down into his eyes. She gave a hoarse laugh.

'Have you been waiting long?'

Mik just nodded.

'Sorry again. My time-keeping's so bad. Haven't got a watch.'

Mik got another hug then. It made him go completely giddy.

The car smelled of wet dog. Lena started the engine, looked at Mik, ruffled his hair and skidded round the square and out onto the road, sending up a shower of snow.

'Have you got a dog?' asked Mik.

'No. It disappeared through the ice last winter. The stupid …' She shook her head.

'Oh,' said Mik.

'It was caught by the current.' Lena ran her hand over the seat. 'But the dog hair is still here.'

Mik sat in silence as they drove through the snow-covered village. The car rattled and creaked and the fan belt screeched. The houses were dotted about randomly; smoke rose from their chimneys and every one had a satellite dish pointed up into space.

They swung off the road and onto a drive in front of a large yellow house. Two snowmobiles were parked by the steps. There were lights in the windows and people were looking out from behind the curtains.

'Hilma has dementia. She is looked after by her relations. Sometimes she goes missing, and she's just done it again. She got cold and it's affected her lungs.'

They walked into the house without knocking.

'Hello!' called Lena.

Mik hid behind her.

The girl with the birthmark appeared suddenly in the hall.

'Hello, Pi,' said Lena. 'How's your grandma?'

'Being awkward.'

The girl called Pi looked at Mik. More people came out into the hall, Pi's parents and the confused granny. Lena handed over the medication and explained how and when it should be taken.

'Oh, and this is Mik,' said Lena, laying a hand on Mik's head. 'He's going to be living with me for a while.'

'Well, that'll be nice, getting away from Stockholm for a bit,' said the dad.

'Stockholm,' said the confused granny and slapped her knees. 'Stockholm. It's all murder and drugs, murder and drugs. Trouble, nothing but trouble.' She looked like a troll.

Pi pulled on her earlobe and laughed.

Mik ran out and sat in the car. He breathed on the window. His breath turned to ice immediately. He melted it with his hand. He blew out ice and tried to think, but his thoughts froze to death, all mixed up. Was this where he was going to live? People here seemed crazy.

Lena opened the car door and threw a pair of winter boots onto the back seat.

'Look what I've got for you. Pi's grown out of them. You won't survive here in trainers.'

~~~

Lena slowed down and stopped in the middle of a bridge.

'Come and look at the river. It's powerful and … well, I don't know what to call it. It gives this place life.'

Mik got out of the car. He held onto the railing and looked down. His eyes adjusted to the darkness. The water flowed black and sluggish. Heavy, slow-moving eddies among the snow white banks. Vapour rose from the surface. It felt as if the bridge was travelling along the water. As if he stood at the prow of a huge boat, looking down.

'It won't be freezing yet awhile,' said Lena. 'But down by Lake Selet, where I live, the ice has started to form. A few more cold nights, that's all.'

'To think it's flowing, even though it's so cold,' said Mik.

'Yes, it hasn't frozen just because it's flowing. Otherwise it would be ice.'

'I don't want to fall in.'

'Over there is the school. See, Mik? The building we passed before the bridge.'

She pointed across the river.

'That little building?'

'Yes,' said Lena. 'That's where you'll be going.'

'I'm freezing.'

They got into the car again and drove on.

'Twelve pupils, thirteen with you.'

'In the class?'

'No, in the whole school. You start on Monday.'

'There's four hundred of us in my school at home.'

'You're in the country now, way out in the wilds. The furniture factory has shut down, the school is threatened and Konsum is probably going to close in the spring. And where are we going to do our shopping then?'

'At ICA,' said Mik.

'Here you either shop at Konsum or you shop at ICA. You don't hop between the two. You're either an ICA person or a Konsum person.' Lena laughed.

Mik saw a man chopping wood in the dark and a dog on a long rope, barking. It raced along the road, following the car until it came to the end of the rope with a jerk. Mik watched through the rear window as the dog flew up in a somersault and fell down onto its back. It's probably dead, he thought. Nothing would survive a yank like that; it's like being hanged.

'That's Gustavsson's dog,' said Lena. 'That leash he keeps it on is far too long. It chases cars and has been run over seven times and is now brain damaged and savage. It was a fine dog, but Gustavsson has ruined it. He got it from me, a puppy from my dog.'

'That died,' said Mik.

'Yes, that died.'

Mik thought that was just as well but didn't say so.

They swung into a front drive and stopped outside a blue house. At least it looked blue in the darkness. Three wrecks of cars, without windows or tyres, stood covered in snow. One had a door missing; another had no bonnet.

'This is where I live.'

'Good,' said Mik. 'Lots of cars.'

'They've got to go, but I use them for spare parts to keep this one going.'

Mik picked up his bag.

Lena looked up at the sky. 'It's a clear night. It's going to be cold. Minus twenty-five, at least.'

~~~

The bed was comfortable and clean, the sheets a bit stiff and frayed. A soft mattress and a cool, thick duvet and three feather pillows.

It was so quiet, no traffic blaring, no commuter trains clattering. No video shop, no pizzeria, no people yelling on the street. Nothing. Only a bus leaving every Thursday.

It was so quiet that for the first time he heard the sound in his head. It was a faint rushing, like the sound in a shell. In his right ear was a low, almost inaudible tone that came and went.

Had it always been there?

He turned onto his side. Blue light from the moon lit up the small room. The walls were covered in dark red wallpaper with a medallion pattern, and the ceiling was low. It was an attic room with a bed, a desk, a chair and a chest of drawers. Nothing more. It smelled nice.

He had noticed it as soon as he had come into Lena's house. It was a kind house and untidy everywhere. There were books all over the place, huge piles that threatened to topple over. They were on the floor, on the table, on shelves and in boxes and bags. Had she robbed a library?

Lena seemed a bit odd. She had no TV, no computer, not even a radio. And naturally she had no DVD or video player. Only books.

To think it could be this quiet.

He folded back the duvet, slid out of bed and sat by the window. The snow shone blue and sparkled a little in the moonlight. Lena's house was on a hill. Far away in the distance there were mountains covered in forest. The village lay in a valley where the river formed a lake, called Selet. The place he had come to was also called Selet. It took its name from the lake.

Smoke was rising from the chimneys, but no lights shone from any of the windows. The houses slept, breathing gently. A little village and then forest, forest, forest. The two closest houses below were exactly the same. A high fence ran between them, as if one of the houses couldn't tolerate the other one. A kick sledge was parked outside each one, at the foot of the front steps.

Which direction was home? He recognised the moon. But that was all.

A peculiar round bird landed high up in a birch tree. But was it a bird? It looked more like a little troll. A flying troll? No, it looked more like an animal than a bird. Although birds are animals too. But this one was –

The stairs creaked. Mik turned to look at the door. No one could creep up on him here in the attic. He would be warned. But if the stairs creaked and no one came … it was haunted. The footsteps had almost reached the top. He looked at the door handle and thought, if someone comes and the stairs don't creak, then it's a ghost.

The door handle was pushed down, the door opened and Lena came in carrying a tray with two cheese sandwiches and a big glass of milk.

'You haven't eaten all day. All you've done is travel. I forgot that.'

She put the tray on the desk and crouched down beside Mik at the window.

'It's lovely, isn't it?' she said in the darkness, quietly so as not to spoil all the loveliness. 'I love this village. It's small and everyone knows everything about everyone. Well, they think they do. I've lived here for seven years and I'll probably stay.'

'There's a flying troll sitting in the tree. Should it be doing that?'

Lena laughed. 'No, it's a hawk owl. It usually sits there. It comes for a while late every evening. It's keeping an eye on me, seeing if everything is as it should be. Then off it flies again. Eat up, now.'

Mik took one of the sandwiches, chewed and looked at the owl.

A light went on in one of the houses behind the high fence.

'Here's Bertil coming out with his potty.'

The door opened, a man came out onto the steps and emptied the potty on a heap of snow beside the door. Then he went back in again.

'He pees badly,' said Lena. 'Little and often.'

'Hasn't he got a toilet?'

'Yes.'

'But why does he pee in a potty?'

Lena gave a quiet laugh in the darkness. 'I don't know. He's just like that.'

The light went off, and a moment later a light went on in the other house behind the high fence.

'Now Bengt's coming out with his potty.'

The door opened and a man came out onto the steps and emptied a potty onto the snow heap beside the door.

'Does he pee badly too?' said Mik.

66

'Yes.'

'And has a toilet and is just like that, him as well?'

'Yes,' said Lena. 'They're twins, but they haven't spoken to each other for thirty years.'

'Why?'

'Old men. It's probably some elk hunt or piece of forest or fishing rights they can't agree on. And that can take several hundred years to resolve.'

'Now I understand,' said Mik. 'I saw the same old man twice today. He went into Konsum with fish, then I thought he came back with fish for ICA. But there were two of them.'

'Yes,' said Lena. 'The Selström brothers.'

'Who piss badly,' said Mik.

'Yes, and the only difference is that one of them is slightly crazier than the other.'

Lena laughed again. She laughed often. Mik liked that, and she smelled nice too. He ate up the last sandwich and drank the milk.

'Right, now you must go to sleep. It's school tomorrow.'

The hawk owl had gone. Mik hadn't seen it fly away. He got into bed and pulled up the heavy duvet. Lena picked up the tray.

She turned around in the door and said, 'It's nice having a boy in the house.'

They looked at each other silently for a while. She smiled.

'The moon up there and a boy here in this room. That's nice.'

NEW AT SCHOOL

Mik woke up and at first didn't know where he was. Then a grinding, stomach-churning anxiety set in.

School. He was the thirteenth pupil.

They would tear him apart. Rub snow in his face. There was certainly plenty of snow to do it with. And he would get an ice ball in each eye. He got dressed and went downstairs.

Lena was crouching in front of the wood-burning stove, getting a fire started. She was feeding the flames with books. She threw in book after book. Then she closed its brass door.

'It'll soon be warm.'

'Books?'

'I've read them, and a book is only something while it's being read. A book is something that happens in your head.'

Lena held up a book and went on, 'And then all that's left is paper. And they burn well and it's warm for a while.'

'Where did you get all the books from?'

'Inherited them from my crazy mum. Three thousand of them. I counted. They'll keep the place warm all winter.'

'Have you read all the books?' Mik looked round at the piles and boxes.

'No, far from it. But a lot of them are the same. Love, murder, that kind of thing. And lots of them are really awful, so they've got to be burnt up straight away.'

'How do you know if you haven't read them?'

'You can feel it when you hold a book. Here, feel.' Lena threw a book at him. 'Is that good or bad?'

Mik weighed it in his hand and looked up at the ceiling. 'Bad.'

'Chuck it in the stove, then.'

Mik opened the brass doors and threw in the book. The pages flapped and the fire caught hold immediately. It was a dry book.

It wasn't far to school. The slippery slope down to the road junction, right at the main road and over the bridge. He would have time. If he hurried. It was minus twenty-two degrees. Lena had lent him a large red ski jacket, an ugly woolly hat and an old pair of knitted mittens. Steam came out of his mouth. The cold stung his nose and neck.

An old woman on a kick sledge went past and then a car with a trailer full of logs. Mik trudged along the side of the road where the snow was deep. The boots felt like massive army tanks and were filled with two layers of socks. If he had worn these on his feet at home his life would have been made a total nightmare. Bigboots. Bootboxes. Bootroots.

He looked up and came to a sudden halt.

There sat Gustavsson's dog, attached to its rope. It glared at Mik and gave a low growl. The dog was a dirty white colour, big and looked like a wolf. Mik stood perfectly still and realised he wouldn't be getting to school. He hated dogs, and this was the only road to the bridge. And how long was the dog's rope? How far did it reach? Could it get as far as the bridge?

They stared at each other, weighing up the situation, calculating. If he ran over to the other side of the road and up onto the ridge of snow pushed against the fence by the snow plough, it might work. But if it didn't work he would be trapped against the fence. It was too high. He wouldn't be able to climb over.

Evil, pale-blue eyes stared at him, following his every move. A gurgling sound came from the dog's throat and its lips twitched. It showed its teeth and said, 'Look what I've got. And what have you got? Little wimp.'

Mik stood in his boots.

Time passed. He was going to be late. His first day and already late. Mik prepared himself and ran. The dog immediately started chasing him. The barking ripped at his ears. The animal was going to get him, grab him by the throat. They always went for the throat. Mik scrambled up the heap of snow beside the road. He heard the yelping, and the rope whistled. He sank into the snow. It was a trap. He fell and rolled out into the icy road, slipped and tried to go faster, but his legs only spun and his thigh muscles burned. Fell again – shit. Rolled onto his back and raised his hands. Protected his neck and got ready to kick. The dog took a powerful leap and hung in the air above him.

Now it would be death by dog.

There was a whip-crack and the beast flew backwards with a sudden jerk. It hurtled round in a somersault and let out a suffocated whine. So that was how long the rope was.

Mik shuffled back on his elbows, stood up and brushed off the snow. The dog slunk away with its ears back, throwing a look over its shoulder.

'Bloody mongrel,' said Mik. 'Go and die.'

All the pupils were sitting in their places. Twelve of them, all ages, but all in the same class. The teacher looked as old as the school. She stood with Mik in front of her and put her wrinkled hands on his shoulders. He wriggled free.

'This is Mik. He is going to be in our school for a while and you must be as nice as you can to him.'

Everyone stared. Unfamiliar eyes. Some grinned; others glared. Mik looked from one to the other. He wanted to go home.

Pi sat by the window. She smiled and pushed her ears forward with her fingers. Waggled them.

The teacher rested her hands on his shoulders again.

'Now you must tell the class a little bit about yourself.'

Mik wriggled free again and stood there in silence.

'But there must be something you can tell us about yourself?'

'My name is Mik and I am … bloody small for my age and only my ears are growing.'

Pi laughed out loud and the rest of the class joined in.

Mik stood stiffly with a fixed expression. Let them laugh.

It had been said: his ears had been betrayed. If they were going to tease him they'd have to find something else. And as far as the boots were concerned, they all wore the same. You wouldn't survive here in trainers. Here you lived in boots.

'We don't swear,' said the teacher.

'Sorry, Miss.'

'Anything else? I'm sure many here are curious about you.'

It went quiet. Everyone waited expectantly for him to say something. A chair scraped, a pen fell to the floor, someone with a runny nose sniffed.

'I'm going to break the world record for holding your breath,' said Mik. 'At the moment Peter Hirvell from Germany holds the record without hyperventilating or using oxygen. The record is six minutes and three seconds.'

'Well, well,' said the teacher.

'Over six minutes?' said a boy with freckles. 'I don't believe that.'

'My own record is three minutes and five seconds. If I survived, that is. I'm not sure about that.'

'Obviously you survived,' said the teacher. 'You're standing here.'

Mik looked around.

'Maybe this is a parallel world.'

'That sounds interesting,' said the teacher. 'You can go and sit down now, next to Pi. She will help you get the right books and so on. You will have to try and find your level in maths and English. I don't know how much you know and how far you had got in your school at home. But I'm sure it will all sort itself out.'

Mik sat down and Pi leaned against him and whispered in his ear, 'You're funny.'

'Me?'

The first lesson wasn't a problem. They were allowed to draw while the teacher read out loud from a book. Mik drew a hawk owl.

During the first break, Pi and her friends gathered around him. Pi pointed first to one, then to another and said, 'This is Filip, with the freckles. He's moody and he's snotty.'

'No-o,' said Filip and wiped his nose on his jacket sleeve.

'And this is Oskar. His brain is as curly as his hair. That's why he's cross-eyed. The curls have tangled everything up so his eyes cross.'

'I'm called Mik,' said Mik.

'We know that,' said Filip. 'And your dad's an alcoholic. That's why you're here.'

Mik took a step backwards. 'That's not true,' he said.

'Everyone knows,' said Filip. 'He's in a clinic and you're here. We know your mum's dead and you're a problem child. Stockholm's full of problem kids.'

'I haven't got any problems,' said Mik.

'Why are you here then?' said Oskar.

Mik shrugged.

'Three minutes and five seconds,' said Filip. 'I don't believe that.'

'Parallel world?' said Oskar.

Mik looked from one to the other. Filip grinned, bent over and filled his arms with snow. Oskar circled Mik once. Looked him over from Lena's ugly hat down to his boots. The predators were out and sniffing their prey. Now he was going to get snow rubbed in his face. Get an icicle in the eye, or …

Pi took a step forward and stood close to him. She was a head taller and looked down into his eyes. She said nothing; her eyes just drilled into his.

Mik felt weak, but he would not give in. Never. But those eyes, there was something about them. His stomach sank. And the third eye, the one that looked right through him. Was it hypnotism, or did he have a temperature? He was actually shaking. Maybe he had caught a cold while standing for such a long time in the square waiting for Lena – or was it something else? A disease that only existed up here in the forest, that all newcomers got? Or was it something she was doing?

Pi suddenly bent towards his shoulder and sucked his earlobe into her mouth. A powerful shock ran from his brain and down through his entire body, bounced around his testicles and out into his legs, only to ping up to his brain again. He stopped breathing.

'Look how red he's gone,' said Filip.

His heart raced.

Pi let go of his earlobe and looked at him. 'He's not breathing.'

'Look, he's turned blue.'

Mik fell.

He was far away in another world, spinning. He lay in a warm ocean, rolled gently by the waves. A few fish swam up and stared at him. Red and blue, some stripy with pointed mouths. Others with soft, round lips. He sank deeper and saw the sky up above and the sun sent down a drapery of gold into the water.

Mik came round with Pi's face close to his. She was blowing air into his mouth. The air smelled of strawberry bubblegum. He lay perfectly still with his eyes closed and heard Oskar say, 'Is he dead?'

'Please breathe,' said Pi. She filled her lungs with air and blew into his mouth again.

He felt her tongue against his. Touched it. Pi backed away. 'He's alive.'

Mik opened his eyes. The bell rang.

THE TABLET MURDERER

Mik walked over the bridge and his footsteps felt unbelievably light. All of him felt light, as if he was filled with oxygen. Something had lifted, somehow. He leaned over the railing and spat into the water, kicked some clumps of snow down and watched them sail along with the current. Then he ran over the bridge.

'Woof.'

Mik stopped, his boots skidding.

The brain-damaged dog sat waiting for him, its cold, pale blue eyes staring. Its mouth opened and closed, gurgling coming from its throat.

'Die,' shouted Mik, and ran.

The rope whined. The dog came level with him. Its jaws snapped shut right behind him.

CRACK.

The dog flew up in an arc and landed on its back.

There was a hole in Mik's thermal trousers. The dog loped back. Mik hurled a lump of packed snow after it but missed. The dog growled without looking at him.

Old man Gustavsson came out onto his front steps and yelled, 'What are you doing? Are you being cruel to the dog?'

'I hate dogs,' shouted Mik and ran.

'I hate children.'

Lena was baking cinnamon buns. The whole house smelled of newly baked buns. She gave him a plateful and he tucked in.

'I'm not much good at baking buns,' said Lena. 'Haven't done any baking since … I don't know when.'

'You're good at buns.'

'How was school?'

Mik chewed a mouthful of bun and then swallowed. Took another one.

'I was funny. Look, I've drawn an owl.'

He showed her his drawing and she thought it was very good. She pinned it up on the hall wall beside a photo of a dog.

'Is that Gustavsson's dog?'

'No.'

Mik looked closely at the photo. It looked exactly liked Gustavsson's mad dog.

'That's Decca. My dog.'

'Was it as nasty as Gustavsson's dog?'

'No. Gentle but bonkers. She often chased things that weren't there. Barked and rushed around. I think she saw spirits in her head. Although sometimes I did actually think Decca saw things no one else saw. Then one day she chased something out onto the lake.'

Lena shook her head.

'I couldn't stop her. She went right through the ice out

there in the middle and was taken by the current. I found her later that winter, way down the lake. She was lying under the ice, frozen solid. The school was having one of its skating days and I was helping out with the barbecue and things. I skated a bit myself and there was Decca, underneath the shiny ice. Looking beautiful, just as if she was alive. It was terrible. Bengt hacked her out for me; I didn't want to leave her lying there. And then I burned her in the back garden.'

'What? You burned the dog?'

'There was so much frost in the ground and it doesn't disappear until the beginning of June.'

'What do you mean, frost in the ground?'

'The ground gets frozen solid. It's impossible to dig. You can't bury anything.'

'You burned the dog?'

'Is that awful?'

'No, it's just … I don't know. You burn books and you burn dogs.'

Lena laughed. 'When you've finished eating you can run an errand for me.'

Mik nodded, his mouth full of bun. Lena put a red box and a blue box on the table. The boxes had small compartments with transparent lids with M, Tu, W, Th, F, Sa, Su written on them. It reminded Mik of trays of fishing flies. In each compartment there were tablets, and Mik realised the letters were the days of the week.

'These are Bengt's and Bertil's tablet dispensers, to make sure they take their medication when they should. Would you take them down to them? Then I can finish baking.'

'Yes.'

'Take a bag of buns for each of them. Bengt lives in the left house and has the blue box, and Bertil in the right house has the red one. You can go straight in, without knocking.'

Mik hesitated on Bengt's steps. Go in without ringing the bell? That felt strange. Could you really do that? That was almost like breaking in. He looked around. The pile of snow beside the door was yellow with frozen pee. He wouldn't want to fall into that.

Of course he had to ring. You can't just walk straight into people's houses. They could be … well, naked or asleep. Back home in Solna you phoned first and asked if it was okay to come round. Then you went round and rang the bell. That meant the person who opened would have had time to tidy up and hide all the empty bottles.

Mik looked around the door frame. There was no doorbell. He knocked with his knuckles, lightly to start with. No one opened. He knocked a bit harder. There was complete silence. Then he thumped hard and heard a faint voice.

'Who's that idiot banging on my door? Come on in.'

Bengt sat at the table in the cluttered kitchen, doing a crossword. Dipped a roll into his coffee and mumbled, without looking up at the visitor, 'Papyrus boat. Two letters?'

'Ra,' said Mik.

Bengt looked over the top of his glasses.

'Ra?'

He lowered his gaze to his crossword and wrote.

'Well, I'll be damned; that's right. I've been sitting here for an hour thinking papyrus bloody boat. Ra. That solves the down word, too. Priest.'

It was stuffy and a bit smelly in Bengt's kitchen. On the draining board lay three pike, staring with rigid eyes. A clock with a gold pendulum ticked on the wall and below the clock was a wall-hanging with a picture of elk.

'I've got cinnamon buns here from Lena and your tablets.'

'Put them on the draining board.'

Mik set them down beside the pike.

'Big fish,' said Mik.

'No, only tiddlers.'

'Bye then.'

'Bye bye,' said Bengt, not looking up from his crossword. 'You going in to Bertil?'

'Yes.'

'Don't listen to him; he's off his head.'

'Does he sell pike to ICA?' asked Mik.

'Yes.'

'And you to Konsum?'

'Yes. But he's a poacher, blast him.'

Bertil didn't have a doorbell either. Should he simply go

in? Should he knock? He stood there on the steps, hesitating. Could he just leave the bag of buns and the tablets here on the steps? No, that would be silly. He lifted his hand and the door opened. And there stood Bertil. He looked like Bengt, but thinner. Bushy eyebrows and a fat nose.

'You're knocking. You don't have to. You can come straight in.'

'But I didn't knock. I was thinking about it, that's all.'

'Perhaps that's enough.'

Mik followed Bertil into the kitchen. It was neat and tidy and smelled clean. The washing-up had been done. Otherwise it was exactly the same as Bengt's. The wall clock hung in the same place. Same rugs, chairs, table and kitchen sofa, except everything here was more colourful. Below the clock was a wall-hanging with elk.

'It's all about synchronicity,' said Bertil.

Mik put the bag of buns and the tablet box on the table. 'What's that?'

Bertil stared at him. 'It's a more profound interconnection that we still don't properly understand. There are simultaneous occurrences apart from those based on cause and effect. It's about time and space connecting in a meaningful way.'

Mik had no idea what the old man was talking about but it was probably best to agree. He nodded and said, 'I've put the buns on the table.'

'There is a crossroads where a number of factors coincide to create something new. One moment in time is completely wrong, another completely right. We are dealing with factors that exist beyond our divisions of time, space and matter.'

'Precisely,' said Mik. 'The buns are on the table.'

'Oh, buns. Very nice. Then I'll put the coffee on. Want a cup?'

'No, I've got homework to do. Bye.'

On the way home, Mik started to wonder if he had got it right. Had Bengt been given the blue box and Bertil the red? Or had he given them the wrong ones? Perhaps Bengt had been given the red box and Bertil the blue? He wasn't sure. Did it matter? Suppose Bengt took a tablet meant for Bertil, and Bengt's tablets made Bertil ill, or …

No, they'd got the right boxes, thought Mik. I ought to be able to manage a simple thing like that. Two boxes in two different colours. But if it was wrong, would it make that much difference? All the tablets in the compartments looked the same, after all.

Maths homework, not a lot. He sat in his room and tried to do the calculations but thought mostly of Pi. 'You're funny,' she had said.

He liked her saying that. He liked the fact that she saw him like that.

He had been given the sums for homework so that his teacher could see how much he knew, where he was up to. Idiotic sums about Lisa buying four and a half kilos of cheese, and Claes mixing orange squash for everyone at a party and how much squash everyone got in their glass.

Mik managed to do most of the calculations, even though it was hard to concentrate. He kept a watch through the window to see when the Selström brothers would empty their potties. They hadn't done it yet. Imagine if they were lying dead in there. Perhaps he had made a mistake with the boxes after all.

He tried to remember, to visualise the colour of the box he put down beside the pike at Bengt's. It was first blue in his mind, then it was green and eventually red. He had forgotten now who should have had which.

They'd better come out soon and empty their potties.

Dead, perhaps. Poisoned by tablets.

Mik tried to count but could only see the old men swallowing tablet after tablet.

M, Tu, W, Th, F, Sa, Su.

The next sum was: Sven has a full tank of petrol in his red car. The tank takes 62 litres. He drives until he runs out of petrol. How far has he driven? The car uses 0.76 litres for every ten kilometres.

Think if they were lying in their beds, pissing blood and writhing about in the throes of death? The tablet murderer had arrived in the village.

He tried to sit still and do the sums one after the other. Stina who bought strawberries. If a litre costs twenty-four kronor how much does seven-tenths of a litre cost?

His skin crawled. He felt sick, wanted to throw up. His stomach was in knots as if someone was rotating an ice drill in there. He felt tablet-poisoned. How could the brothers be able to empty their potties if they were lying dead in their houses?

Mik leapt up so fast the chair tipped over. Rushed down the stairs and past Lena, who was washing up.

'Where are you going?' she shouted, but he was already outside.

He ran and slid down the road and raced in to Bengt, who looked up from his crossword, bewildered.

'Have you taken any of those tablets? I think you got Bertil's. I think you're going to die.'

'Ugh, those pills. I don't take them anyway. I throw them away. Do you know a reptile with thirteen letters? The first letter is N and the fifth from the end is O.'

'Nile crocodile.'

'Good. That makes six down cryptography. Secret writing. You're a devil at crosswords. Have you been taking lessons or something?'

Mik looked at the tablet dispenser on the draining board. It was blue. He felt totally confused.

'Should you have the blue box? Have you got the right one?'

'Oh, yes. But don't tell Lena I don't take the pills. She'll only start to get awkward.'

THE CAT FACTORY

Mik woke in the middle of the night. It was the song that had woken him. Long, drawn-out notes. The sound rose and fell. A beautiful song, but sad. It went quiet for a moment but then it started up again. Faint, melodious sounds rose up, only to die down.

Where was it coming from? He looked out of the window. Yes, it was coming from Lake Selet. The lake formed by the river in the middle of the valley between the mountains.

Last night steam had been rising from the water, but there was none tonight. The song came from the lake. Mournful tones. Whales? It sounded like the whale song at the museum. Could there be a lone lost whale in the lake? The sound was magical and the whole snowscape out there was like a fairy tale. All the small houses lay in the tranquil, blue light of the night. And far, far away in the distance rose the high black mountain. The mountain of primeval mountains, beyond the river of primeval rivers.

The hawk owl landed in the tall birch tree.

Could there really be a whale in Lake Selet? How had it got there? In Loch Ness in Scotland there was a sea monster from prehistoric times. Did that mean there could also be a whale here? An ancient whale from prehistoric times.

The light went on in Bengt's kitchen. He came out onto the steps and emptied his potty on the pile of snow. The hawk owl flew away. Bengt remained standing there for a while, looking down over the lake, then went in and switched off the light.

~~~

They were doing maths in school. The teacher corrected Mik's homework.

'Traffic jam?' she said. 'What kind of an answer is that?'

'Well, it depends on the traffic how far Sven goes in his car. It might be in the middle of rush hour with queues and red lights, so he wouldn't get anywhere even if he had a thousand litres in his tank.'

'But there wasn't a traffic jam,' said his teacher. 'The car uses zero point seventy-six litres every ten kilometres, so all you have to do is multiply that by the number of litres in the tank.'

'I know,' said Mik.

'Well, then, why have you written traffic jam?'

'I was trying to be funny.'

'In maths you don't have to be funny, and we don't have rush hour up here. It's sixty kilometres to the nearest traffic lights.'

During the lunch break Mik sat on his own on the climbing frame. It was the middle of the day but the sun was low and pale in the sky. There were hardly any days here at all. The sun only said a quick hello over the mountain tops and then it was gone again. The cold was like your actual North Pole. Minus twenty-two degrees. If it was this cold back home they didn't have to go outside at break time. If it was this cold at home they didn't even have to go to school.

A girl came up and stood in front of him, staring. She was wearing an ugly fur hat that looked like a dead beaver. Mik glared back. He didn't know her name.

'I've never seen traffic lights,' she said.

Mik didn't answer.

She took a step forward.

'I've never been on an escalator. Is it fun?'

'Like being in a lift, more or less.'

'I've never been in a lift,' she said and ran off to her friends.

Mik looked around for Pi and saw her in her bulky red jacket, telling Oskar and Filip something. He wanted her to see him. Pi was obviously saying something funny. She waved her arms about and everyone laughed.

Mik took out his mobile and made an important call to Peter Hirvell, asking him how he prepared for his underwater record. Peter Hirvell said something amusing and Mik laughed so that the whole playground heard. Filip, Pi and Oskar walked over. Mik ended his phone call.

'Bye then. Call you later.'

'What a massive old mobile you've got,' said Filip and took out his. It had a radio, MP3 player, camera and everything.

Pi and Oskar showed them their mobiles. They also had a camera and MP3 player but no radio.

'Mine's a video camera too,' said Filip. 'Can I see yours?'

He took Mik's phone and cradled it in his hand as if it weighed ten kilos. He pressed a few buttons and looked at the display.

'It doesn't work.'

'Battery's dead,' said Mik.

'Mine lasts a hundred hours, at least.'

'Huh,' said Pi. 'It doesn't matter what kind of mobile you have.'

'Yes it does,' said Filip. 'Look, I've got a torch, too.'

'Mine's got a bigger colour display,' said Oskar.

'You can't get it wet, though,' said Filip. 'Mine's waterproof.'

'Mine won't break if you drop it from high up,' said Oskar and dropped it onto the frozen ground.

The battery popped out and the display cracked. Oskar was very, very upset. He managed to slot the battery back in. Half the coloured screen was black.

'Genius,' said Filip.

Pi sprinkled some snow on Mik's hat and smiled.

'You coming to Konsum to buy some sweets?'

Filip protested. 'Oh, why does Traffic Jam have to come?'

'Because he's funny,' said Pi.

'I haven't got any money,' said Mik.

'I have,' said Pi and brought out a thick wad of notes and some coins from her pocket. It was a surprisingly large amount.

'Shall we buy him some?' said Oskar.

'Yes, let's do that.'

In the square between Konsum and ICA a few men were putting up a big Christmas tree.

'I'm going to ask for a new mobile for Christmas,' said Oskar.

'That's nothing,' said Filip. 'I'm getting a snowmobile.'

They went into Konsum. Oskar gave Mik a shove.

'And what do you want?'

'I don't know.'

'What do you mean, you don't know? Haven't you written a list?'

'No, but last Christmas I got a hockey stick and … a puck.'

'A puck!'

Oskar fell about laughing.

'You're hilarious.'

They lined up in front of the sweet containers, each holding a bag. Mik put a few sweets in the bottom of his, some marshmallow bananas, sour fruits and chocolates. He looked at Pi who had scooped her bag full.

'Puck,' said Filip. 'Hockey stick and puck? You've got to write a list.'

Mik looked down into his bag and wondered if he dared take any more.

'A Christmas present list,' said Oskar. 'With the best things at the top. At the bottom you throw in some boring things, like a warm jacket or something.'

'I'm not putting anything boring on my list,' said Filip.

'Who do I give the list to?' said Mik.

'Are you being funny or are you just thick?' said Filip.

'I never usually write a list,' said Mik.

'Yeah, and that's why you got a puck … for your hockey stick.'

Pi took Mik's bag from him and peered into it. 'What's this?'

'Some marshmallow bananas and …'

She gave him back the bag.

'Fill it to the top. I'm paying.'

On their way out they stood in the warm blast of air between the doors and looked at the notice board. Mik ate his marshmallow bananas and read the cards about logs for sale. He read about studded tyres for an old Saab, a lost sledge and a meeting in the community centre to discuss the wolf situation. And all those lost cats. Something that wasn't there last time Mik looked at the notice board was the card about the fishing conservation organisation holding its annual meeting. Everyone was invited for coffee and saffron buns.

'I can't see any change,' said Oskar.

'Yes,' said Mik. 'Saffron buns.'

'What are you talking about, saffron buns?'

Mik pointed.

'There, at the fishing meeting. Everyone gets buns.'

'We don't care about buns,' said Oskar. 'We've got other things to –'

Filip shook his head and pulled a face at Oskar.

'Oh, nothing.'

'What?' said Mik.

'Nothing for you to worry about,' said Filip.

Pi laid her hand on Mik's head.

'He can be in on it.'

'No way,' said Filip. 'There'll be less each if we have to share. And he won't be able to keep his mouth shut. Why does he –'

'Because I want him to,' said Pi. 'Mik won't say anything. He's okay.'

Filip stared moodily at Mik who had his mouth full of marshmallow bananas and didn't have a clue what they were talking about.

The disused furniture factory was a large brick building beside the river. The windows were covered with pieces of wood, nailed into place. Oskar and Filip opened a metal hatch beside the factory chimney. Pi grabbed hold of Mik, twisted him round to face her and held him by his ears, staring deep into his eyes.

'You must promise on your life not to say a thing.'

'Yes,' said Mik.

'On your life.'

'I promise on my life not say anything.'

'Good.'

'What am I promising not to say?'

They crawled into the hatch and along a narrow shaft and came out inside the factory. Pi switched on the lights. The fluorescent tubes on the ceiling hummed and flickered. All around stood carpentry benches, planes, drills and saws. The floor was covered in wood shavings. On a table was a coffee cup with the dried remains of coffee inside. A newspaper lay open. It looked just as if the workers had gone for a break and would soon be back.

'My dad worked here,' said Oskar. 'But they make furniture cheaper in China.'

Mik smelled something strong and pungent. The whole factory stank of cat piss, and he saw a cat sitting on a shelf, washing itself. Further away on a workbench another cat was lying down, sleeping. Fat and white. Suddenly there were two, rubbing themselves against his legs. There were cats everywhere. It was a cat factory.

'We have a business idea,' said Pi, picking up the white cat. 'We look after the cats until the reward is right.'

'Business idea?' said Mik.

'Yeah, don't you get it?' said Filip. 'These cats have run away. The owners want them back, but it'll cost them.'

'Course I get it,' said Mik.

'They're all right here,' said Pi. 'The heating's on low so the machinery won't be damaged.'

'The machines are going to China,' said Oskar.

'And they get cooked fish every day,' said Pi. 'Synchro-Bertil gives us all the small pike.'

Oskar found Greta's cat, a tabby with white paws. He stroked it and said, 'You've been missing long enough. Your owner thinks you're worth three hundred kronor. You're a real goldmine.'

Pi pointed at another cat with grey, matted fur.

'It's called Nisse and has been here for ages. He's bad business. It's Crow-Lasse's cat. He hasn't even put a card on the notice board. But we have learned a few things. It's important to know who the owner is before the cat goes missing. Old ladies and families with little children are best. Old men are useless. They're not bothered about their cats. They shouldn't be allowed to have cats.'

Mik picked up a black cat with yellow eyes.

'We should never have taken that one,' said Filip.

'Why not?'

'It's Maria's cat and she's ... '

Filip went silent. No one said anything. Mik looked questioningly at the others.

'What's that about Maria? Who's she?'

'Nothing,' said Pi.

The black cat purred.

Greta lived in a yellow house a stone's throw from the church. Pi carried the cat in her arms. They stood outside on the road and looked towards the house. Filip and Oskar practised their story. How, where and when they had found the cat.

'In the forest,' said Filip.

'That's no good,' said Pi.

'In the forest, caught in a fox trap,' said Oskar.

'That's better,' said Pi. 'But not good. Too complicated.'

'In a tree,' said Mik. 'It was sitting high up in a tree and couldn't get down. Meowed and cried.'

'What?' said Oskar. 'You mean it's supposed to have been sitting up in a tree for two weeks?'

'How do I know when it climbed up?' said Mik.

'That's good,' said Pi. 'In a tree. We don't know what it did before that. Maybe it climbed up there a few hours before we found it.'

'Yes, but where was it before that?' said Filip.

'How are we supposed to know that?' said Pi. 'We've only just found it, and that's all we've got to say. It'll only get complicated otherwise.'

Greta, an overweight woman with bright red cheeks, was so happy to see her cat again that her eyes filled with tears. She cradled the cat in her arms, rocking it like a child.

'Come in, come in. Let me give you something to drink and some cinnamon buns. Sit down and I'll lay the table.'

She let the cat down, clapped her hands and began busying herself in the kitchen. The cat was given food and a saucer of cream. Buns and cakes appeared on the table.

'How clever you are,' said Greta. 'You found her last summer too. Where did you find her?'

'At the top of a tree,' said Pi. 'Mik had to climb up and get her.'

'In a tree?' said Greta, astonished.

'She was probably lost in the forest before that,' said Filip.

'Shut in a fox trap,' said Oskar.

'What?'

Pi glared at Oskar.

'We found her in a tree; we don't know about anything else. She might have been shut in or lost or anything.'

'What would I do without you?' said Greta and bent down to stroke the cat. 'It's Christmas soon and it would have been so empty without her.'

'The money,' said Pi.

'Oh yes. The reward.'

Greta pulled open a drawer, lifted up a book and took out three one-hundred-kronor notes from underneath.

They took a short cut through the graveyard towards the school.

'You nicked the cats,' said Mik.

'We're making people happy,' said Oskar. 'We're doing something good. They would never have been this happy if the cat hadn't got lost and then found again.'

'How are we going to share the money?' said Filip sulkily, wiping his nose on his sleeve. 'There are three one-hundred-kronor notes and now there's four of us. That's three divided by four. It's far too complicated.'

'I don't need to get any money,' said Mik.

THE WELL OF STARS

Lena threw a few old encyclopaedias into the stove, solid bricks with leather covers.

'How was school today, then?'

'Cool,' said Mik.

'What shall I make for dinner?' said Lena. 'We've got sausages. Shall I cook some macaroni?'

'No, I'm full up,' said Mik, looking down at his last marshmallow banana, which was twisted and grubby in his fingers. 'We found Greta's cat today.'

'That's good. I expect that made her happy.'

'Yes, it was sitting up in a tree and I was the one who had to climb up and get it. No one else dared.'

'How clever! You can do another good deed. I've collected Bengt's new reading glasses. Will you run over with them?'

Mik didn't knock; he simply opened the door and stepped right in. It felt like breaking and entering. Bengt stood with a fork in one hand, frying bacon. The smell filled the whole kitchen.

'Hello. I've got your glasses.'

'Put them on the table. Want some bacon?'

'No thanks.'

Bengt ate straight from the frying pan with the fork.

'Do you know how to fish?' he said, a hot piece of bacon sticking out of the corner of his mouth. 'Have you ever fished for pike?'

'No.'

'I've caught thousands. Konsum Lasse and I export to France. There's a place that appreciates pike. Fine food. No one eats pike here any more.' Bengt chewed his bacon.

'Are they big, pike?'

The frying pan was empty. Bengt put it in the sink.

'Do you want to come fishing with me and help check the lines?'

'Yes.'

'Come down at six o'clock tomorrow morning. Wrap up well.'

Mik turned in the doorway and said, 'There's a whale in the lake.'

'What?' said Bengt, looking doubtful.

'I heard it sing.'

'That was the ice you heard. The ice sings when it's settling. It's the pressure.'

'Whales sing too.'

At precisely six o'clock next morning Bengt stood with his sledge, waiting for Mik. On the handle hung a bucket of roach and in the pike box lay a large axe.

'Sit in the box and I'll get going.'

They took the quick route down to the lake and out onto the ice, where there was no snow. The sledge glided quickly and easily through the darkness. Its runners whooshed and their cheeks stung from the speed. Strange glowing lights flickered over the sky. Magical green and yellow curtains.

UFOs, Mik thought, but Bengt said calmly, 'The northern lights. It's the earth's magnetic field meeting the solar wind.'

Lake Selet was big, bigger than it looked from his attic bedroom window. Not very wide, but long.

Bengt stopped. 'Here's my first hook.'

It was a hole hacked in the ice with a stick resting across it and a line attached to the stick. Bengt used the axe to hack at the ice that had formed overnight, then felt the line. It jerked in his hand.

'Oh, yes, we've got one. Not too big, but lively.'

Bengt pulled a wriggling pike up onto the ice and hit it on the head with the back of the axe. He baited the hook again with another roach that he had killed first by throwing it onto the ice. It was cruel, he said, to bait the hook with a living roach.

'Yes, if it's dead it can't be in any pain,' said Mik. But he thought, if it's dead then it's dead.

'Roaches don't understand anything anyway,' said Bengt. 'They don't even know they exist.'

'But think if it does, and the pike too.'

'Jesus chose fishermen for his disciples. This kind of cruelty is allowed.'

They glided over the ice to the next hook. Bengt chopped away the thin ice, felt the line and looked at Mik.

'This is a big one. Do you want to do it?'

Mik nodded and Bengt gave him the line. It swung heavily and the tugs were frighteningly strong.

'Hold on,' said Bengt. 'Show who's in charge.'

Mik looked down into the black water. The line moved round and round in the hole, scraping away ice at the edges. Suppose it wasn't a pike? Perhaps it was something quite different. Anything at all could be down there in the dark water. Bumps and jerks could be felt on the line; something was tugging hard. Something wanted to pull him down into the darkness. There was water on the ice; it was slippery, and he slid towards the hole.

'Put some effort into it,' said Bengt. 'If you can only get him to turn his head up, he's yours. But you have to be quick before he turns away again.'

Mik pulled. The line rushed round and round. It was a tough battle.

'You've got him now, only the last bit left.'

Large wide jaws appeared in the hole. Teeth and a yellow eye with a black pupil. The jaws smacked in the air and hissed.

'A dragon!' shouted Mik. 'It's a dragon.'

'Now, pull the line over the ice and he'll come up nicely.'

The pike slid up over the edge and slithered about on the ice. Swam without getting anywhere. It was enormous and its back was as thick as a giant python. Bengt hit it over the head with the axe. The pike quivered and then lay still. There was blood on the ice and Mik stopped cheering.

'Put it in the box.'

Mik lifted his catch. It was heavy. Imagine if Tony could see him now. Imagine if Tony could see what an incredible ice dragon he'd caught. There was not enough room for it in the box. Its head and tail hung out.

The next two hooks were empty. There were only the pale roaches staring with dead eyes.

'Look,' said Mik, pointing across the ice. 'There's someone over there.'

In the dim light they saw a dark figure on a kick sledge.

'That's Bertil,' said Bengt. 'He's got his hooks along the other side. Blasted poacher. These are my waters.'

Muttering, Bengt steered the sledge to the next hole.

Mik slid about on the ice. It was all shiny and flat. He lay down and stared through it. Trapped, frozen bubbles hovered like planets. He put his tongue against the ice. It was cold and tasted of nothing. Then he stood up, ran for a bit and then skidded along on the soles of his boots. The glide was fantastic. He ran and skidded with his arms outstretched to keep his balance. Further and further out. He was just about to pick up speed again when he felt something strange. Bouncing. Mik looked down at his feet.

The ice was moving, in waves. Immediately in front of him was open water. A perfectly round hole in the ice, a few metres across, filled with black water. Like a huge well. The northern lights and the stars glimmered on the surface. A perfect mirror image of the sky. He moved carefully, went a little closer. The surface swayed and the image of the sky buckled and twisted. It looked as if the stars were hovering deep below the water. A well with stars in it. He went carefully closer, his feet gliding. The tiniest movement and small waves trembled over the edges, as if the well was speaking to him, answering his movements.

How deep was it? How far down were the stars? Endlessly far away? As far down as it was up to the sky.

'MIK!' yelled Bengt over the ice. 'Get away from there! It's dangerous, you could die.'

Mik stared down into the well of stars. Backed away carefully.

'There are stars here,' said Mik. 'There are stars down there.' And then he thought he saw something huge move past in the dark water.

Bengt stopped the sledge and waited at a safe distance.

'Be thankful you're so small and light, otherwise you would have been dead by now. There are strong currents out there and the depth of the lake bed suddenly changes from eight metres to three. The current is treacherous and you don't stand a chance. It'll pull you under the ice. You'll be dragged far away up the lake and stay there until spring, staring up through the ice.'

'Like Lena's dog?'

'I hacked Decca free a kilometre further up. And I don't want to do the same with you.'

'I saw something massive. I saw a whale. Stars and a whale.'

'There's nothing there. You saw the sky, the northern lights, and you've got to watch out for that swift water hole. Now you know where it is. Later in the winter even that will freeze over, but only thin ice. Then you can't see it so you must know where it is.'

'How?'

'Take your position from the high ridge on the other side and the church up towards the village. Then the mast up there on the mountain and the boat-house. If you're standing where those points meet, you're in trouble.'

Bengt removed his mittens, undid the belt around his waist and slipped off his sheath knife. He handed it to Mik.

'Here, take this knife. You can have it. It has saved me when I've fallen through. You stab it into the edge and pull yourself up.'

It was a fine knife with a bone handle and a leather sheath.

'Promise you'll always have it in your belt when you're out on the ice.'

Mik promised.

They drew up the remaining lines and headed for home. The box on the seat was full of pike. Mik stood on the runners in front of Bengt. On the horizon there was a thin blue line over the mountain. A weak dawn that struggled and pushed against the black sky.

'Don't say anything to Lena about what happened at the ice hole. That you were out there.'

'I won't say anything.'

'Good.'

In school, during break, Mik told Pi how he had caught the big pike. The others stood around them and listened. He showed how he had pulled as if his life depended on it, because at any moment the pike could drag him under the ice. A dangerous fight, which the pike was winning. A battle of life and death.

'That's cruelty to animals,' said the girl who had never been on an escalator.

'No, Jesus fished for pike.'

'Where?' said Filip. 'Here in our lake or what?'

'I don't know where they fished.'

'You're disturbed,' said the girl who had never been on an escalator.

'Go on,' said Pi. 'I want to hear.'

Mik continued his battle with the pike that had now become a dragon.

'An ice dragon!' he shouted. 'And then I fell into the hole but got myself out, hanging on to it by its neck. It bit me and I bashed its head in with the axe.'

He whirled round and round to show them, lay in the

snow and writhed and hit out. Imitated the death throes of the dragon. Rubbed snow in his face and then lay motionless in the snow, arms and legs outstretched.

Pi laughed, but Filip said, 'You're lying.'

'Who cares?' said Pi. 'He's good at telling the story.'

'What?' said Oskar. 'You mean you can lie as long as you're good at telling the story?'

'Yes,' said Pi and pulled off her mitten, crouched down and stuck her hand under the ear flap of Mik's hat. She rubbed his ear lobe between her index finger and her middle finger.

He turned hot all over. They looked into each other's eyes. She smiled.

Mik thought the snow had melted all around him and he had trouble breathing. Pi rubbed; Mik turned redder.

'He'll be fainting soon,' said Filip.

'He's holding his breath on purpose,' said Filip. 'To show off.'

'He looks funny,' said Oskar.

The bell rang. Pi let go of his earlobe, put on her mitten and ran.

'Don't get any ideas,' said Filip. 'She'll keep you as her little pet.'

Mik gasped for air and thought, I'd give anything to be her pet, or anything else of hers.

～～

It was late. Both Bengt and Bertil had done the evening's last potty round. Mik took a piece of paper and wrote CHRISTMAS LIST at the top. The light was off and he was sitting in the blue darkness. Mik looked at the words, bit his pen. Doodled in one corner, raised his head and looked out of the window. The hawk owl sat in the tree and the northern lights flickered. The solar wind swept across the magnetic field. Magical curtains in the most amazing colours drew across the sky.

Mik sat for a long time with the piece of paper in front of him without being able to write anything. What did he want? The hawk owl ruffled its wings, preened its feathers and flew away over the houses where the Selström brothers lived. Mik put pen to paper and wrote. But who should he give the list to?

Father Christmas?

God?

Or Tengil?

He looked out through the window again. The sun storm had drifted past. The stars were shining behind thin, hazy clouds.

The stairs creaked. Lena came in with milk and sandwiches. She put the tray on the desk.

'I could hear that you were awake. Are you doing your homework in the dark?'

'No,' said Mik, putting a hand over his sheet of paper.

'Are you writing letters?'

'No.'

105

Lena leaned over the desk and saw the capital letters of the heading.

'I see. Is it what you want for Christmas?'

'Maybe.'

'Exciting,' said Lena and tried to snatch the piece of paper.

'No,' said Mik and held on to it.

'Well, if it's a Christmas list I've got to see it. You'll be here over Christmas, and I'm the one who'll be talking to Santa Claus.'

She smiled and Mik let go of the paper. Lena read, 'I want Dad to stop drinking.'

She stood in silence, not knowing what to say. The stairs creaked. They shouldn't have done, because no one came up.

BRAVE AND SCARED

It was the Christmas holidays. Mik was eating his breakfast, looking out of the window. The snow was falling heavily. You could hardly see the houses where the Selström brothers lived.

A yellow snowplough with a flashing orange light thundered past on the road outside. Lena was seeing to the wood stove. She put in several armfuls of books.

'Today it's dirty books for pensioners.'

'Dirty books?'

'Books with naughty bits for old ladies.'

'That doesn't sound too good.'

Mik was in a hurry and ate his sandwiches quickly. He was going to meet Pi, Oskar and Filip at the cat factory. Maria's cat was going to be found. The reward had been increased from one hundred to two hundred kronor.

'By the way,' said Lena, shutting the stove doors, 'they rang yesterday to say you're going home two weeks after New Year.'

'Home?' said Mik, his mouth full of bread.

'Yes, that's when school starts.'

'Who's "they"?'

'Her, that woman from social services.'

'Parrot Earrings?'

'She said that –'

'I don't want to go home,' interrupted Mik. 'I want to stay here.'

Lena filled the coffee pot with water and placed it on the stove.

'It's all right with me if you stay.'

'Then I'll stay.'

Lena measured coffee into the pot.

'It's probably not that simple, but –'

'I'm staying,' said Mik, clearing the table.

He put on his outdoor clothes fast. Hat, mittens, boots, thermal trousers and the enormous red ski jacket. Dressed for landing on the dark side of the moon. Dressed to survive the next ice age. Dressed to go out of doors in a village called Selet, by a lake called Selet.

'Where are you going?' said Lena.

Mik hesitated, his hand on the door handle.

'It's a business idea.'

'Exciting. What is it?'

'We find things.'

'Such as what?'

'Cats.'

'Well,' said Lena. 'Goodness knows we certainly need cat finders. Every cat in the entire village seems to have run away. Yesterday Åkerlund's disappeared. Their youngest daughter is really upset.'

'I'm sure we'll find it,' said Mik.

'Come home at lunchtime. One o'clock would be good.'

Home, thought Mik as he walked through the falling snow. He missed Tony; of course he did. He missed Ploppy. He missed the smell on the staircase in the flats.

The snowflakes fell in their thousands, millions, billions. He walked with his face looking up at the sky and poked out his tongue. The flakes landed, cold, and melted.

Home?

He didn't miss his school. He didn't miss Lisa Nordahl and her sweaty green chair. He didn't miss the clink of bottles. He didn't miss Solna Swimming Centre. The list of what he didn't miss could be made long. He had decided. He had moved here. Left home. Parrot Earrings could say what she liked. Dead or alive, he wasn't going to leave here.

The snowflakes made him dizzy. He lowered his gaze and there stood Gustavsson's dog. Mik crouched down, took off his mittens and made a handful of damp snow.

'You want an ice ball in the eye?'

~~~

Maria's house was the drab colour of faded wood and was on the outskirts of the village. The chimney leaned and a few roof tiles were missing. The TV aerial was rusty. There were no curtains in the windows, no pot plants, nothing. The windows were only empty staring holes. There was no satellite dish.

Pi held the cat in her arms.

'You've got a hole in your trousers,' said Oskar.

'I missed,' said Mik.

'What?'

'With the ice ball.'

Filip stood silently, looking as if he had a mouth full of red ants.

'What's up with you?' said Pi and gave him a shove.

'We should never have taken her cat.'

'What do you mean?' said Pi. 'It got lost. We've found it; we're good at that.'

'I'm not going in,' said Filip.

'Then you can forget about the money,' said Pi.

'I don't care about the money. She's totally mental. It's a haunted house.'

Filip's mobile started ringing. He answered and said he had to go home to eat.

'How very convenient,' said Pi. 'What are you having? Baby food?'

'I'm not scared of anything, but my lunch is actually ready.'

Filip left. Oskar kicked hesitantly about in the snow and said, 'Do you have to go in to get the money?'

'Yes,' said Pi.

'But if I stay out here and wait, what do I get then?'

'A hatful of snow,' said Pi.

'Then I'm not doing it either.'

Oskar ran and caught up with Filip and they disappeared into the falling snow.

Mik realised that now was his chance to show Pi how brave he was. He mustn't let it go by. Whatever he had to face in that house, he would not flinch. He would stand up straight and die, if necessary.

The hall was large and dark. A wide staircase wound up to the first floor. Weird pieces of string ran the length of the walls.

'Hello!' said Pi and continued walking in.

The string criss-crossed every room as if a mad person had put up several miles of washing line.

Or a spider, thought Mik, a spider that has made an enormous web. There were things hanging from the strings. Dried flowers, perhaps, or some kind of fruit. It was hard to see. He entered a large room and looked for a light switch but couldn't find one.

Pi had disappeared and he hurried to the next room. There stood an old woman wearing a peculiar dress covered with embroidery in gold and red.

'Hello,' she said, smiling.

They weren't flowers hanging in the strings. Mik screamed. They were dead pigeons hanging in bunches, tied by the feet. Bouquet after bouquet of dead, dried pigeons which made your skin crawl and your leg muscles twitch.

'Pigeons,' said Mik.

'No, angels,' said the woman. 'I catch angels.'

Mik shot towards the door. He got tangled up in the strings. Tore at them, was trapped and fell. Feathers floated down around him and he got a mouthful. He spat, hissed and whirled his arms. Made it to the door and threw himself out.

He didn't stop until he had come to the main road. He filled his mouth with snow, washing his tongue free of feathers. But he couldn't get rid of the disgusting taste. It was as if he had chewed on a mummy. Bloody hell, how he had run! Pi would hate him now. He was a coward. He had missed his chance.

Mik looked up towards the house and waited. After a while Pi came out. She had the reward money and handed a hundred-kronor note to Mik.

'No, I don't want it,' he said, fishing in his mouth for a feather that was stuck under his tongue.

'You're brave,' said Pi.

'No. I got scared.'

'You can actually be scared and brave at the same time.'

'Can you?'

'Yes. Being a coward is something else. You came with me. That's enough.'

LETTER TO TONY

Lena poured hot soup into a thermos.

'Bengt has gone through the ice.'

'What?' said Mik. 'Has he drowned? Has he …?'

'No, Bertil saved him. But only in the nick of time. He was in the water for ages. Would you run down with the thermos?'

Bengt was standing in his long johns, hanging wet clothes to dry above the stove. He swore and muttered and didn't say hello. Mik pulled up a chair so he could reach the cupboard. He took down two bowls, poured out steaming hot soup and handed it to Bengt.

'It was snowing so hard I couldn't see a blasted thing. I went the wrong way and suddenly I was in the ice hole. Crack, and there I was in the water. I've done it before but this time I couldn't get myself out.'

'The knife?' said Mik.

'You had it. I forgot to put another one in my belt.'

'But it turned out okay,' said Mik. 'Bertil saved you. You're alive.'

'OKAY?' roared Bengt, like an angry bear. 'OKAY?'

There were waves in the soup. Mik stood horrified and silent. Bengt held out his arms.

'I would rather have drowned than be saved by him.'

'Why?' said Mik.

'Don't you understand?' said Bengt, shaking his head. 'Now I owe him my life. I'm in debt. Hell, I feel sick just thinking about it.'

Bengt removed the wet long johns and hung them above the stove. He stood naked in his kitchen. Blew his nose in the palm of his hand.

'This is the worst bloody day of my life.'

'Here, eat your soup,' said Mik.

~~~

The evening was clear, with northern lights. The storm had passed over. Brightly coloured drapes rippled against the sky. Mik sat in his pyjamas at the desk and bit his pen. The hawk owl came to rest in the tree.

Mik put his pen to the paper and wrote.

Hi Tony,

I have never written a letter before. Where do I start? I have caught a dragon. It was strong and almost dragged me down under the ice. But I won. Now it's on its way to France to be eaten in a posh restaurant. School here isn't like school at home. Because everyone from first grade to sixth is mixed together in one class because there aren't enough children to make more classes. The teacher is old and it's very forbidden to swear anywhere near the school, which might be closed. Then we won't have to go. There's a girl in my class. She's called Pi and she's great. Filip's a bit mouthy, but he's a coward. Oskar's fun, but he's afraid. None of them dared to go into Maria's house when we were going to give back the lost cat we had taken. We hide them in the factory until the reward is right. And I got a dead pigeon in my mouth. Auntie Lena is nice. She has burnt her dog and she burns books. I'm going to burn Gustavsson's dog. Bengt went through the ice and was saved by Synchro-Bertil. They are brothers but haven't spoken to each other for thirty years. I think there's a whale living in Lake Selet but Bengt doesn't think so. He has trouble pissing. So does Synchro-Bertil. There's a flying troll that sits in the tree outside the window. Konsum is going to be shut down. Then Lena will have to shop at ICA instead. But she says she'll never do that, because here you're either a Konsum person or an ICA person. There's no pizzeria, video shop, underground, commuter trains, traffic lights or escalators here. It's weird. Even Bengt and Bertil have got a satellite dish. Without a satellite dish you can only get TV2. The forest mountain is in the way.

Mik read through the letter. He had included everything and thought it was a good letter, considering it was his first. But he added,

I'm staying here. Lena has promised I can.
    Pi's ...

Mik looked out of the window, fiddled with the pen and thought. She's … What kind of words were there? He had suddenly come into an area that was completely unexplored on the map, empty of words. He wrote,

> She's good. I like her.
> How are you? Bye,
> MIK.

The stairs creaked. Lena came up with sandwiches and milk. Mik put his hand over his letter.

'Are you writing a new Christmas list?'

'No, it's only a letter. To Tony.'

'Right. I can post it for you.'

'I'm going to forget about that list. It's childish. Only small kids write to Father Christmas.'

'I don't go in for Father Christmas, either,' said Lena, putting down the tray. 'All that Christmas stuff isn't my thing.'

Mik picked up a sandwich, started to eat and said, 'I don't go in for Christmas either.'

Lena laid her hand on his head and ran it tenderly down his neck.

'Promise never to go out onto the ice.'

'All right. But I can go fishing with Bengt, can't I?'

'Of course, but not alone. And always in warm boots.'

Lena thought for a moment and changed her mind. 'But he did go through the ice himself, so …'

116

'Bengt's big and heavy. I don't weigh anything. And he didn't have a knife.'

'Okay then. But never alone.'

'I promise.'

FATHER CHRISTMAS
SMELLS OF PIKE

It was Christmas Eve and Mik realised he was going to miss the Disney Hour on TV. But that didn't matter; he'd seen it plenty of times before. But even so, an orange, and Donald Duck and Mickey Mouse, and Chip 'n' Dale, and Jiminy Cricket – wasn't that the moment Christmas happened, when Jiminy Cricket sang?

Lena didn't have a television. They had talked about that.

'Do people have to have one?' said Lena.

Mik thought for a while and decided that probably people didn't. He wasn't entirely sure. But it was odd. Everyone had a TV. It was like not having a toilet, or a cooker, or clothes.

'It's a matter of principle,' said Lena. 'Neither TV, radio or newspapers are going to determine my daily routine.'

Mik wasn't actually sure what Lena meant but he knew he was missing Donald Duck.

'You can go down to Bengt at three o'clock,' said Lena. 'He's got a huge flipping TV. But first we're going to make pizza.'

There were other things, too, that were different and odd. There were no Christmas decorations in the house. No tree, no tinsel, no Christmas elves, no angels, nothing. Only ice patterns on the windows. They were pretty and a sign that it was terribly cold outside. They spread upwards on the windows when the temperature fell to minus twenty degrees.

'I suffer from Christmas psychosis,' said Lena. 'I feel panicky and get a kind of allergic reaction to houses full of Christmas hysteria. The whole Christmas thing makes me ill.'

'Why?'

She thought for a moment, then shrugged.

'Rotten Christmases when I was a kid.'

'I got a hockey stick and a puck last year.'

The phone rang. Lena answered and had a short conversation, hung up and turned to face Mik.

'Hilma's burnt herself making toffee. It's not a major problem, but would you run over with some salve?'

Mik pulled on his thermal trousers and boots, his ski jacket, mittens, hat and scarf and stepped outside into the silent cold winter landscape.

He felt like an astronaut equipped to withstand minus two hundred degrees. He looked around, took out his mobile and held it in front of his mouth like a walkie-talkie.

'Astronaut on distant ice planet reporting to the mother ship. Everything is sparkling white and the ground is creaking under my feet. You can breathe the air if you're careful. Steam is coming out of my mouth. No other signs of life here. Oh wait, yes, now I see a space alien. What is he doing? Well, he's emptying a potty. Base, can you hear me? A space alien emptied a potty. Do you require me to take samples?'

Base did not require that, so Mik requested to be beamed up.

There was something wrong with Gustavsson's dog. It was sitting in front of its house, facing the wall. On its head was a red hat with a white pompom, held on with an elastic band, and under its chin hung a white beard. It turned its head and threw a long, ashamed look over its shoulder.

'Happy Christmas!' shouted Mik.

The dog whimpered faintly and turned to face the wall again.

The whole of Pi's house was red. Red and hot. It smelled of food; it smelled of oranges; it smelled of toffee. It smelled of Christmas Cola that had frothed over. And Christmas music blared from the radio. In every window were stars and candles. The curtains were red, the tablecloths were red and Pi was dressed in a red dress with a red ribbon in her hair. Her grandmother Hilma was red too, and the hand she had burned was bright red.

'Come and look at the tree,' said Pi.

It stood in the middle of the floor with gold tinsel, red baubles, angels and elves. Presents were piled under it. Mik felt he would faint from overheating in his astronaut suit, or perhaps he was about to faint because Pi looked so incredibly beautiful there in front of the tree. Her white smile in the middle of all that red.

She straightened her dress, took a few dance steps in front of him and stretched out her hands towards the tree.

'Isn't it lovely? I decorated it myself.'

The house was full of people. Cousins, second cousins, uncles, aunties. The little children were prodding and shaking the presents. The house vibrated with expectancy.

'We've made a snow lantern that's shining out there,' said Pi, dragging Mik to the window.

He came up close to her. She smelled good. He was filled with an overwhelming desire to creep in under the Christmas tree, take Pi with him and live there for the rest of his life. To creep in under this Christmas and stay forever. It made him go dizzy. His brain was filled with a red, twirling shimmer and in the middle of all the red Pi's mouth laughed. Red lips with white teeth. He had become red-blind.

Pi's mum danced into the room. 'Come on, kids,' she said, 'Let's dance round the tree.'

Grandma came in and started dancing and the radio belted out 'Here comes Santa Claus, here comes Santa Claus'.

'Don't want to,' yelled the children, rummaging among the presents.

'But Grandma thinks it's fun,' said Pi's mum. 'Come and dance now, for her sake.'

Grandma twirled around the tree, whee-heeing and whoo-hooing, and frightened the smallest child, who started crying.

Mik went out into the hall and Pi followed.

'I'd better go now,' said Mik and looked over Pi's shoulder at several men standing in the kitchen, drinking.

'You can stay if you like.'

'No, I've got to get home. Donald Duck and …'

'Do you want some toffee?'

She gave him a whole bag and bent forward and kissed him on the mouth.

'Happy Christmas,' she said, and he staggered out into the cold as a kind of mist filled his head.

Gustavsson's dog was still sitting facing the wall with the Santa hat on its head.

'Have you got Christmas psychosis?' shouted Mik.

Bengt had a china Father Christmas on his kitchen table, but apart from that there was no sign of Christmas. His TV in the best room was silver and unbelievably huge. It didn't fit in with the odd assortment of furniture in the crowded room. It looked as if it had travelled through a hole in time and landed here.

Mik sat on the floor and Bengt sat in the armchair. The picture was amazing, almost like the cinema.

'Super Trinitron tube,' said Bengt. 'Seventy kilos. Got it cheap now everyone wants flat screen TVs. Do you know how many channels I can get?'

'No.'

'Fifty-one, but that's including Turkish and Albanian and who knows what bloody else.'

'That's a lot,' said Mik.

'But I watch videos mostly. Doris Day. See, on that shelf? I've got videos of all her films.'

'Doris who?'

'We can watch one some evening,' said Bengt and put down a bowl of nuts. '*April in Paris* is best. What a woman!'

It got to three o'clock and Disney Hour. Chip 'n' Dale were mean to Pluto and Donald Duck was angry in the jungle.

'He's funny, that crazy bird,' said Bengt.

But he didn't like Ferdinand the bull sitting under the cork oak tree.

'Someone ought to chop down that bloody oak.'

The bull smelled the flowers.

'He's gay.'

But Bengt thought one of the picadors was funny. It looked like Bertil.

Baloo started singing.

'This is the best one,' said Bengt and sang along for a few lines until he got the words muddled up.

Bengt was all right, thought Mik. Bengt was just being himself. There was nothing else hidden behind there. Nothing that would suddenly jump out and scare you. Bengt said he thought like a pike, and what he meant was that he always knew where, when and how they should be caught. But he probably thought more like Baloo. He was actually quite like that stupid jungle bear.

Christmas flickered from the super Trinitron. Robin Hood stole the king's money and during *Lady and the Tramp* Mik suddenly thought of Pi. He knew very well why.

When you wish upon a staaaaar, makes no diffcrence who you aaaare. The candle melted. And that was the end of Christmas Eve.

'Now you must go home and wait for Father Christmas,' said Bengt and switched off the television. 'I've got a difficult crossword puzzle to solve.'

He got up out of the armchair stiffly, coughing badly. He cleared his throat and said, 'Then we can go fishing early tomorrow morning. You're going to catch the big pike.'

'I'm too old for Father Christmas and I haven't asked for anything.'

'Not asked for anything? What do you mean? Everyone always wants a load of rubbish. It's all about using up the world's resources to make brightly coloured toys. That's the meaning of life. And here you are, not wanting anything. What's going to happen then? The whole machinery will grind to a halt. The stock exchange will crash. People will lose their jobs. Suicide and worldwide depression.'

'I don't want anything.'

Bengt laughed.

'Are you a communist?'

~~

Outside it was dark and the stars twinkled in the sky. No wind, no sound.

124

Light streamed from every house. There were fairy lights in garden trees, strings of rope lights flashing along house roofs. Shining Father Christmases in the gardens. Flashing Happy Christmas signs. The whole village sparkled like a firework in the winter darkness. And over there, on the other side of the river, the forest began. No troll would dare make its way to the village on such a night. Mik sang, 'When you wish upon a STAAAAAAARRRR.'

He shouted, 'When you're fishing from AFAAAARRRR.'

Then he yelled with all his might, 'When you wonder where you AAAAARRRGGGHHH!'

Gustavsson's dog began to bark and Synchro-Bertil opened his door and came out onto his front steps.

'It's Christmas,' he said.

'Yes,' said Mik.

'Want a cup of coffee?'

'No thanks.'

'Well, Happy Christmas, then.'

'Happy Christmas to you.'

Mik and Lena lit candles, ate pizza and didn't wait for Father Christmas. They burnt books and played board games.

'We'll honour this day by burning classic literature,' said Lena, putting a pile of books in the stove. 'August Strindberg, and here's a Joseph Conrad but it's a bad translation. Then I think we'll have some Hemingway with our mulled wine.'

'Mulled wine?'

'It's alcohol-free, so you can have some.'

'No.'

Lena looked at him. The table was full of candlelight that glittered in her eyes. It was lovely and calm; everything was all right. Nothing would happen. Nothing could happen. Lena leaned across the table and ruffled his hair. The candle flames flickered.

'My dad drank too,' said Lena. 'He was also an alcoholic and around Christmas he would be drunk for several days. One year, when I was ten, he got so drunk and mad that he wanted to shoot my mother. He had a shotgun. Something just snapped in his head and we were chased down into the cellar. My big brother protected Mum. He stood in front of her. I wet myself.'

'Did he shoot?' said Mik. 'Did he shoot your brother?

'No, Dad lowered the gun and went. He fell asleep in front of the TV and we hid the weapon. After that he was dead as far as I was concerned. Christmas was also dead.'

'But your brother, he was all right, wasn't he? He saved your mum?'

'Perhaps,' said Lena.

'What a brave brother you've got.'

'Yes. He's your dad.'

Mik didn't understand at first. His thoughts froze and trillions of snowflakes fluttered in his brain. Lena was his dad's sister. Dad's sister, but ...

'The worst thing,' said Lena, 'was that my mum also started drinking. They would get as drunk as you could possibly get. I was always worried in case something happened. And Mum hit Dad, and …'

Lena fell silent and stared into the candle flames. Wax dripped down onto the table. She went on, 'That anxiety, it crawled around in my body all the time.'

'The Snake,' said Mik.

'The snake?' Lena looked at him.

'Snake Alone with his back-to front-scales.'

'Yes, exactly,' said Lena. 'Like a snake with back-to-front scales.'

'But …,' said Mik. The thoughts still whirled in his head. '…if the same thing happened to Dad, why does he … Why? I don't understand.'

'It's a curse, things repeat themselves through generations,' said Lena. 'And that snake you mentioned can get very thirsty as time goes on.'

'Did you drink too?'

'Yes.'

There was a knock at the door and they looked at each other in surprise. They sat in silence. There was another knock, then heavy thumping.

'If it's Father Christmas we'll rub snow in his face,' said Lena.

Mik opened the door and it was Father Christmas. Big and fat with a white beard, fluffy fur cloak and a hat.

'Merry Christmas,' he said. 'Has everyone been good this year?'

Santa held out a sack, and he smelled of pike.

'I'm too old for Father Christmas,' said Mik.

Lena came and stood behind him in the doorway. She put her hands on Mik's shoulders.

'Exactly,' she said, laughing. 'We don't believe in you.'

'You can believe what the hell you like,' said Father Christmas and handed over the sack. 'Merry Christmas.'

And he left.

'Father Christmas smelled of pike,' said Mik.

'Mm,' said Lena. 'And I think he has trouble peeing.'

They tipped the contents of the sack onto the floor and started rummaging through the parcels. Two were from Pi to Mik. A cushion she had sewn herself, embroidered with a heart, and a diary with sweet little rabbits on the front. He ought to have thought it was ridiculous, rabbits and a cushion, but he didn't. The cushion smelled nice. From Father Christmas he had a fishing rod and fishing hooks and some sweets. Lena had bed linen and velvet pyjamas from someone called Liz.

'Bought in New York,' she said.

It got late and Lena drank mulled wine and put more Hemingway in the stove. Mik fell asleep in front of the fire on the cushion he had been given by Pi. Lena carried him up to his bed, he was so light. She tucked him in and said, 'It's going to be empty and lonely when you're not here any more.'

She looked sad. That surprised Mik, because he wasn't going anywhere.

He told her, 'I'm staying here. Parrot Earrings can say what she likes. It's nice here. I want to live here. Can't I?'

'Yes, as far as I'm concerned you can stay here.'

'Well, I live here then.'

Lena smiled at him and stroked his cheek.

'Yes, you live here.'

'Promise I can live here.'

'I promise.'

THE ICE DRAGONS

Bengt lay in his bed under a pile of covers, shivering. His cheeks were burning and runny snot dribbled from his nose. He coughed, sniffed and looked up at Mik with eyes that were bloodshot and too shiny.

'I think I'm going to die,' he said.

'You've got a cold,' said Mik.

'A cold,' rasped Bengt. 'This is no stupid cold. It's tuberculosis. I won't be leaving my bed again. My head's all dizzy. I'm freezing to death and I'm boiling hot at the same time.'

'Exactly. You've got a cold. Lena said you got cold in the water. You've got a temperature.'

Bengt stared at the ceiling and then shut his eyes tightly. 'Damn. Can you check the lines and bring in the fish yourself? It's got to be done. The fish will die and go bad … it's got to be done.'

'Alone?' said Mik. Bengt looked at him. Tears streamed from his eyes, but he wasn't crying. He was leaking water.

'You know how it's done.'

'But I've promised Lena never to go out on the ice alone.'

'You've got the knife. Show me you've got the knife.'

Bengt propped himself up on his elbows. Mik lifted up his jacket. The knife hung from his belt.

Bengt lay down again and pulled the sheet up to his chin.

He sniffed and said, 'Get Bertil's too.'

'No,' said Mik.

'He's a blasted poacher.'

'But he saved you.'

'Oh hell, so he did.'

The ice was shiny, the snow had blown away and the sledge glided easily and quickly. The runners crackled and swished and the headwind stabbed his face like a thousand nails. On the sledge seat was the pike box and in the box was the big axe that he would use to kill the pike. Bengt had told him that if he found the first hook he would find the rest, in a north-south direction from Tallåsen. And north was in the direction of the church steeple.

It wasn't difficult. He found it straight away even though the morning was still dark. He cracked the night ice layer with the axe and almost dropped it in when the ice broke open. Mik felt the line. It was heavy. And then it started to jerk and pull. The line rushed around the hole, scraping against the ice edge. He hauled up the line and a big pike floated up, its jaws working.

Mik threw himself at it, hitting it on the head with the axe. The pike died. Mik laid it in the box and travelled proudly on to the next hole. Here comes the trapper travelling through the polar regions, he thought. No, Siberia, catching deadly ice dragons, seven times deadlier and bigger than Nile crocodiles.

Mik looked down into the box. The pike's mouth was open, its teeth bared. A Siberian ice dragon. Deadly. It spits out slime and you can be paralysed and die at the slightest touch of it on bare flesh. It would even make dragon Katla from *The Brothers Lionheart* run off and hide in her cave by Karma Falls.

～～～

Three hooks in a row held ice dragons. Two were small, the third enormous and much bigger than any he had caught with Bengt. It wasn't difficult getting it up onto the ice, just heavy, but then it turned into a battle. Mik lay on the ice and tried to hold it still. The ice dragon thrashed and squirmed, opening and closing its jaws. Mik aimed a blow, but he missed and the axe hit the ice so hard his hand went numb. He fought, wrestled and hit, sat across the pike and managed to strike it several times in the middle of its head. Blood ran onto the ice. The dragon stiffened, spread out its fins and shook as if it had received a ten-thousand-volt shock. It opened and closed its jaws one last time and finally slackened and died.

Mik stood up and cheered across the ice with the axe raised above his head. But then he became anxious in case he had been affected by the slime and paralysis would come creeping, and there was no cure. That was the cruellest thing about dragon slime. Your body fell apart inside and the paralysis slowly set in. Would he make it off the ice in time? Would he get home in time? Would he ...?

Mik decided it hadn't affected him and he carried on to the next hook. Numbers five and six were empty, but the rest held ice dragons. The box filled up and Mik's gloves were wet with dragon slime which froze and turned stiff. It felt like his hands were in plaster, or was it paralysis? Perhaps the gloves had a hole somewhere? Cruel world.

On the other side of the lake he saw Bertil gliding along on his sledge, checking his lines. What idiotic brothers, thought Mik. What could make him and Tony not speak to each other for thirty years? It was mental. There was enough room and enough pike for everybody. Complete madness, actually. But Bengt had told Mik it wasn't madness. It was perseverance.

Mik turned for home and for some reason which was inexplicable even to himself he didn't take the quickest route. He came under the influence of some magic power and went where he shouldn't, straight towards the ice hole. He knew what he was doing, but his will was not his own. Something tugged in his stomach and bubbled up his legs and into his testicles. Out there lay the black patch of open water. It was as if it was calling him. A black eye amid all the white. A black hole with enormous magnetism. There was something there.

The sledge runners hissed. The ice became thin and dark. Trapped, frozen bubbles floated like planets in a black cosmos. Here and there were cracks like frozen lightning in the ice. He stopped the sledge and walked the last bit to the ice hole. The ice bounced under his feet and vibrations caused little waves on the surface of the open water. There was a faint crack. He stopped for a moment, listened. The ice whined, complaining quietly.

One more step.

And one more.

He was close now. The water seemed oily, slow-moving. Small eddies and streams of current glided on the surface. Tears in a single eye. A black, bottomless eye staring up into space, endlessly upwards, endlessly downwards. An entrance into another world. Upwards, downwards, inwards, outwards.

One more step.

How close is close?

How close can you go?

One more step.

The waves lapped around the edge and in towards the middle, where they met and bobbed back again. He was allowed to go everywhere in the whole of Selet, anywhere at all. Apart from here. And this was where he was.

Why was he here? Was it all to do with the bubbling feeling in his testicles? How close could you go?

One more step.

He stood on the edge. The ice wasn't very thick, only a few centimetres. This was close. You couldn't get any closer.

Here he was alone. It felt good. Could you be any more alone than this? This was the edge and no one would follow him here. Mik thought he saw a shadow of something down in the water. Something drifted past. Perhaps it was the current; perhaps it was clouds passing across the dark morning sky.

No, there was something down there. Something massive. Sliding his feet, Mik backed to the sledge.

Bengt was still in his bed, hidden under the duvet. Mik took off the stiff, slimy gloves and brought out a bundle of notes and Bengt's blue tablet box, which he laid on the chest of drawers.

'Here's the money from Konsum Lasse and the tablet box from Lena. I lied to her and said you'd been out on the ice.'

'Keep the money,' said Bengt from under the duvet.

'No, I have money. My own job. Pi and I … find cats.'

'What's the time?'

'Half past nine.'

'I have to get up.'

Bengt crawled out from under the duvet, sat on the edge of the bed and swayed groggily.

'I saw the whale,' said Mik. 'It's there in Lake Selet. In the ice hole.'

Bengt looked at him with bloodshot, feverish eyes.

'You're not supposed to go there.'

'I've got the knife. And I did actually see a whale.'

'That's impossible. And I don't need those pills.'

'Why? Why should everything be impossible? I saw it. In

Loch Ness there's a prehistoric monster. So there could be one in our lake too.'

Bengt lay down in bed again. Sighed and pulled the duvet up to his nose.

'The chances of there being a whale in Lake Selet are unbelievably small. Almost non-existent. Practically zero.'

'You do believe me?'

'No, but I'll keep an open mind. There might be a one in ten million chance that there's a whale in the lake.'

'One in ten million. But you do believe it?'

'What would it be doing in there?'

'Magnetically lost,' said Mik. 'So you do believe in my whale?'

'I believe your whale means something.'

'So then you believe?'

'Yes, in the meaning.'

AN ICE BALL IN THE EYE

The Christmas holiday came to an end. It had been good. It had been the best Christmas holiday ever. They had handed back six cats. He and Pi had built eight gigantic snowmen when the weather turned milder after New Year. One was four metres tall and was admired by everyone in the village. Mik felt as if he had helped create a masterpiece. Bengt's temperature dropped to normal and he helped them put the top half of the huge snowman in place. Oskar thought they ought to ring the *Guinness Book of Records* so they could put the snowman in their next book.

'It's not that big,' said Filip. 'I bet they've built bigger in Alaska.'

Parrot Earrings had phoned three times and spoken to Lena. Mik had told Lena to tell her he had moved for good, that he had left home and now had a new home. This was home and he had no plans to leave.

The weeks passed and the days became longer. The sun did more than say a quick hello over the horizon. It hung up there, and some days there was no need to put on a thick hat at break. The school had sent for a whole box of hockey clubs and brand new goals. They played all break time and Mik was goalie on Pi's team.

She was best, but Filip thought he was best. He wasn't. He was the moodiest. Oskar had a tooth knocked out by his own stick when he was about to shoot into an open goal. That was exactly the kind of thing only Oskar could do.

Filip had been given a snowmobile that no one had seen. It was either being serviced or lent to a cousin or at the garage for tuning.

It was evening and the hawk owl sat outside in the tree. Lena came up with milk and sandwiches. Mik had a peculiar pink shimmer in his brain. He didn't know what it was. But he was happy and the happiness kind of ran out of his ears, nose and mouth like pink candyfloss. He bounced on his bed on his knees in his pyjamas and asked, 'Why do you put your tongue in someone else's mouth?'

Lena laughed. 'Well, because you like that person.'

'The one whose mouth you put your tongue in?'

'Yes.'

'Good.'

'Why can't you ever hang up your clothes?' said Lena and realised she was starting to sound like a mum.

Mik's clothes lay in a crumpled heap on the floor. He looked at the pile. Socks, trousers and jumper lay there just as if the person who had been wearing them had gone up in a puff of smoke or suddenly shrunk to the size of an ant. Lena hung the trousers over the chair and money fell out of the pockets. Coins and crinkly notes. She stood there, astonished.

'Lots of money. Where did you get it from?'

'Earned it.'

'Doing what?'

'We've got a business idea. A cat factory. Pi and –'

'Cat factory?' said Lena, counting the money. 'There's six hundred kronor here.'

'Yes, it makes them happy.'

Mik felt the candyfloss flow out of his mouth. Everything was going so well. His body buzzed and he jumped around on the bed on his knees. She could know. She was all right.

'They've run away. We look after them until there's a good reward.'

'What?'

'The cat owners are really glad.'

'You look after them?'

'Yeah, until the reward is good.'

'You kidnap cats? That's …'

Lena looked strange. Was she angry or what?

He stopped right in the middle of his bouncing. The candyfloss shrivelled up and stuck all around his mouth. He shouldn't have said anything. You should never say anything.

'But the cat owners are so-o-o glad. They would never have been that happy if the cat hadn't been lost and we'd returned it to them.'

'That's not right, Mik. But go to sleep now; we can deal with it later.'

Lena went down the stairs. Mik pulled his duvet up over his head. Why did he have to babble on like that? You should never be that happy, because it only bubbles over. How bad was this?

It took two days. Then he knew. It was bad. Shit, it was bad. It was crap bad. Vomit bad. It was as if a great big bulldog had wandered into the village and pissed on him. He needed a time machine. He needed to rewind and start again. Or else he needed a strong rope so he could go out into the forest and hang himself.

Pi looked right through him now. He was so much thin air. She simply walked on by, as if she was walking right through him. It would have been much better if she had hit him, screamed and yelled, rubbed his face in the snow – murdered him. No, he didn't exist, she didn't see him. The only one who had spoken to him was Oskar, and he said, 'I'm not allowed to talk to you.'

And he screwed his mouth up tightly so it looked like a bumhole.

Lena had spoken to all the cat owners in Selet and apologised on behalf of the children, but most of all for Mik, who, according to her, had only been talked into it. Obviously the thing with the cats became the talking point of the entire village.

'Those kids have got a bloody nerve!'

'It's got to be that problem child from Stockholm, coming up with such an idea.'

But Bengt had laughed and told Mik they could be business partners and the idea could be developed a little.

'No,' said Mik.

'Yes, we could sell insurance,' said Bengt. 'Cat owners can insure their cats with us. Anyone who refuses will soon find their cat has disappeared.'

No one else had laughed. In school their teacher talked about right and wrong, about norms, rules and how people ought to behave towards each other. There was group work and Mik was the odd one out and did group work on his own. He wrote an essay about how the plague came to the Nordic countries:

In 1349 a ship came drifting towards the Norwegian coast outside Bergen. It was towed into the town and searched. The whole crew was dead. The bodies were black and blue with boils that had burst. But the cargo was undamaged. It consisted of valuable cloth that was sold and spread across the Nordic countries and one person in three died of the plague.

'Aren't you in a group?' asked the teacher.

Mik looked up from his story.

'Yes.'

'It doesn't look like it.'

The teacher looked around the classroom.

'Mik has to be in a group.'

It went silent. Someone giggled.

Break times were lonely. The hockey game flowed backwards and forwards. Mik sat on the climbing frame. Pi scored a goal and cheered. Filip got angry, threw his hockey stick to the ground and told the goalie what he thought of him. The match continued with shouting, yelling and cheering. Pi knew he was sitting on the climbing frame – obviously, for how else would she have been able to stop herself from looking in that direction?

The ball rolled towards Mik and came to a stop at his feet. He bent down and picked it up. Pi looked the other way. Filip came to get it. Mik held out the ball.

Filip took it and said, 'Your dad's a wino.'

And the game got going again.

My dad's a wino, thought Mik. The words tasted rotten in his mouth. The words tasted of sick. The words tasted sour. The words tasted Snake.

Gustavsson's dog was waiting for him. It growled, curled back its lips and bared its teeth. Mik took off his gloves and warmed some snow in his hands. He made a hard-packed ball of ice. Took his time. The dog started barking and steam poured out of its mouth as if at any moment fire would come spurting out.

Mik took a few steps back and then started running with his arm raised behind him. He threw the ice ball with all his strength. The dog had no time to see it. Smack, it went, right into his eye. He flew sideways, his head in the snow, and stayed there on the ground for a while before he limped, whimpering, from the road. Mik was able to calmly walk past.

'Die,' said Mik.

A silver-coloured car stood in the driveway of Lena's house. Mik didn't recognise it – lots of people came to visit Lena. She was never off duty. People always needed some kind of cream or had a sore throat or had twisted their ankle. It could be all kinds of things. Mik stepped in and was taken by surprise. This was no twisted ankle.

At the kitchen table sat Parrot Earrings and Gold Tooth.

'Well, hello there, Mik,' said Parrot Earrings.

'Hi, how's it going?' said Gold Tooth.

Lena stood with the coffee pot in her hand. She looked at Mik and then at the visitors and then at Mik again. There were buns on a plate. Mik took one, started eating it and decided not to say a word. Nothing. He had moved here and that had nothing to do with them. There was nothing to be afraid of. This time it was Lena who would decide, and he knew he could live here.

Gold Tooth got up and stood by the front door. Why did he do that? Mik's bag stood packed on the floor with Pi's cushion on top. He saw it but didn't understand at first. He stopped chewing his bun and went completely cold. The chill ran up his back, spread over his shoulders and right into his heart. He spat out the bun and yelled, 'NO! I'm not going.'

He turned and ran for the door, but Gold Tooth grabbed hold of him and held him tight.

'But Mik,' said Parrot Earrings, 'your dad's fine now. Of course you have to go home. He's struggled for your sake. He's …'

'I haven't got a dad,' shouted Mik, wriggling in Gold Tooth's grip. 'I haven't heard from him. He hasn't phoned, he hasn't written to me. He doesn't exist.'

'Now you're being unkind and unfair,' said Parrot Earrings. 'This was only temporary.'

'He's a spade.'

'You're going home.'

'I live here,' shrieked Mik. 'I've moved here. Let me go, you piece of shit.'

Lena said nothing. She stood with the coffee pot, as if paralysed, and cried.

PART 3

THE ZOMBIE BOOK

Zombie Book 8/3

How do you write a diary like this? Are there any rules? And what should you write? Are you allowed to write prick? Mik, prick. MIIK. PRICK. MMMMIIIKKK.

Zombie Book 11/3

I've blacked out the rabbits on the front of this diary with marker pen. Because this is no rabbit book. This is a zombie book.

Zombie Book 15/3

Ploppy and I nicked a shopping trolley in Solna today. We rode it down the slope where the swings are. We could have killed ourselves. The wheels were too small so we tipped over. Ploppy scraped his elbows.

Zombie Book 21/3

A zombie is a body with no thoughts or feelings. A ghost is thoughts and feelings without a body.

Zombie Book 25/3

Tony's angry all the time. I don't know what's up. But something's happened. You can't talk to him like before. He's never home. The video shop was on fire. School's been set on fire too. It was Ploppy who set light to the paper towels in the girls' toilets outside the dining-room. There was a lot of smoke for such a small fire. The fire alarm went off and everyone had to run outside and stand in line in the playground. Now they've taken away all the paper towels from the toilets. I had to go and see the principal. It wasn't an interrogation, he said. He wanted to know if I had any information, and I didn't. But I think he thinks it was me.

Zombie Book 27/3

More about zombies: a zombie is made by black magic and voodoo. A sorcerer carries out a ritual that makes someone die. Often it's a very hated person and someone has paid the sorcerer to get rid of them. The body is then called back. But it's a body without a soul and with serious brain damage.

Zombie Book 2/4

I've got a noise in my ear. I can only hear it when everything is absolutely quiet. A noise that lives inside my head. Should it be there?

Zombie Book 3/4

Tony and I boxed today. It was a tough match. Tony said I won, but he gave in. He can do better. But I punched him in the solar plexus. He wasn't prepared for that. My shoulders are blue now. Actually they're the same pattern as the knitting on my jumper. The bruises are small squares.

Zombie Book 7/4

Ploppy and I went to Solna shopping centre at lunch break. It was liver at school and Ploppy and I hate liver. We went to the hot dog place and bought hamburgers instead. Then we nicked some DVDs. No one said anything and we just roared with laughter when we came out. It just happened; it was pure chance. It was like it wasn't me who did it. If it hadn't been liver in school it would never have happened. The films were rubbish.

Zombie Book 12/4

On my bed is the cushion Pi gave me. It lies there looking supernatural. It might just as well be a present from an alien. Here you are, a present made of magic material. An unexplainable thing. A cushion.

Zombie Book 14/4

You hear a lot of wrong stuff about zombies. They're not half-dissolved bodies that shuffle through the night to eat fresh brains. Zombies don't hunt people; they eat normal food.

Zombie Book 15/4

I read about scientist Michael Rockefeller from New York. He was on an exploration to New Guinea and when his canoe capsized, Rockefeller swam ten kilometres and came ashore on a beach where cannibals lived. Since then no one's seen him.

Zombie Book 17/4

Today I saw Lisa Nordahl and sat in her sweaty green chair. I don't understand her. If I tell the truth, she doesn't believe me. If I lie, she believes me. Today I told her Dad and I had gone to Gröna Lund at the weekend. We bought wristbands and went on everything. Freefall and that new big dipper were best. Then I told her Dad had got a new job, and she thought that was good. She was glad, she said, that everything had turned out so well. But he hasn't got a new job. He's washed up on a beach with cannibals.

Zombie Book 18/4

Tony hasn't been home for a few days now. There's not much food left. Heated up a tin of baked beans and watched a programme on TV about air crashes. Most air crashes happen at take off or landing. Only three out of ten happen during the actual flight. That can be a comfort to know while you're up in the air.

Zombie Book 19/4

This evening Ploppy and I broke into a building site and pissed in all the machines. First we drank one and a half litres of Coca Cola. They're building a car showroom right where we had our dens. But we're planning to stop them.

Zombie Book 22/4

Our wall clock in the kitchen has a second hand. It ticks loudly. Today I tried to beat my record. I held my breath on the kitchen chair and stared at the clock. My whole body felt like it was exploding and my ears roared. The seconds dragged by. I fell off the chair. Tried again and again but got rubbish times. There must be something wrong with the clock. It's going too slowly. I put in a new battery but my times were useless. I'm going to train every day. Ate beans. Tony hasn't come home. Going to bed now. The cushion still smells of Pi. To make the really good times you've probably got to be underwater. On land it's too easy to give up.

Zombie Book 24/4

There's a gun here at home. I found it at the back of the wardrobe when I was looking for bottles. I asked Dad and he said what the hell was I doing snooping around and I should stop acting like I was the police. I could go to hell with my bloody snooping. But I know what kind of gun it is. It's a shotgun.

Zombie Book 25/4

There was no pissing on the building site so tonight Ploppy and I went and poured sand into all the tanks. A big van came so we hid. The van stopped by some containers. Three guys jumped out and cut open the doors. Ploppy said they welded open the containers. But that's wrong. You weld things together. You do cutting with an acetylene torch. It was like fireworks. Sparks rained down like from a massive sparkler. Then they loaded things into the van. Tony was one of the three guys. Ploppy didn't see that, but I did. I didn't say anything. We got out of there.

Zombie Book 4/5

Lisa Nordahl wants me to tell her my very first memory. The thing I first remember about my life. When I first discovered I existed. No, I couldn't. I kind of never discovered I existed.

But of course you've got a first memory, she said. But I couldn't remember anything. She didn't give up so I made up a story about how the family was on holiday in New Guinea and the boat sank and we saved ourselves by landing on a cannibal island. She got angry. But she tried not to show it. She said I was lying, and I said that if the cannibal island is my first memory, then it is. It couldn't be, she said, it simply can't have happened. No, it didn't happen, I said, but it's my first memory. And she can't tell me what my first memory is.

Her first memory was walking through a meadow with her grandmother, picking flowers. Barefoot. Harebells and daisies. I refused to believe it. I might have done, if she said she'd stood on a piece of glass or something in that meadow. My dad, I said, he shot a cannibal with a shotgun we've got in the wardrobe at home. Slap in the middle of the forehead, and it made a big hole in the back of his head where his brains flew out. That was the end of our chats for this week.

Zombie Book 6/5

Six ways to detect a zombie:

- Slowness. Zombies move very nervously and slowly. They don't react much or not at all if you try to make contact with them.

- Difficulty speaking. Zombies either can't speak or they express themselves in very short sentences. Although often only with sounds.

- Squinting eyes. Zombies are, as a rule, only awake at night. Their eyes cannot tolerate sunlight.

- White spots on their skin. Zombie poison can be so strong it causes white patches.

- Insensitivity to pain. Zombies can feel pain but they react very slowly and therefore seem insensitive to pain.

Bad smell. Zombies don't bother washing themselves. They are very dirty and tatty and often have rotten teeth.

Zombie Book 7/5

Sand in the tanks didn't stop them building. Why do they have to build a car showroom just where we had our camps? Who's decided that? Tengil?

Zombie Book 8/5

Dad was sitting on the sofa. He wasn't that drunk. Perhaps he'd only had one bottle. He was happy and said we'd go fishing in the summer. He wondered if I remembered the stream and the perch we used to catch.

Maybe, I said, but it was a long time ago.

Well, this summer we'll go fishing, you and me, he said. Dig for worms and use them for bait.

The bottles were behind the sofa, a whole row of them.

Later, after he'd drunk another bottle, he began boasting and talking about when he worked at sea. It makes me want to throw up just hearing about it. Then, after the third bottle, he gets that thousand-metre-deep look, foggy and far off. He doesn't move his eyes, he turns his whole head, as if his entire eye mechanism has gone wrong.

Then comes the crying and how he's going to die. Somewhere towards the end of bottle number four he usually falls asleep. This is when he's been drinking wine. It goes fairly slowly then compared to when he drinks spirits. Spirits are dangerous. You have to be prepared. There's no crying period. He gets angry and violent. He can say I'm a bloody disgusting bloody little creep. He shouts and I'm scared he might go into the wardrobe. Spirits don't make him fall asleep – he crash lands. His brain switches off, all systems shut down, he gets confused. His eyes turn black and then he falls over. Sometimes a soft landing, sometimes hard. I tip away any alcohol that's left over.

He hates me. It's me who's going to make him stop drinking.

Zombie Book 11/5
Crying a lot makes you thirsty. I drink a lot of water.

Zombie Book 12/5
There was a ring at the door today. Parrot Earrings and Gold Tooth were standing outside. I saw them through the spy-hole. I didn't open the door. For a minute I thought about getting the gun. That would have given them a surprise.

Zombie Book 13/5
Wonder if there's any medicine that would kill Snake Alone. Simply kill him there inside my stomach, so I could shit him out.

Tony came home today. I asked him where he'd been and he said he'd moved in with Dennis. I told him about the gun in the wardrobe. Tony just shook his head and tore up the bills. Then he took some clothes and left.

Zombie Book 17/5

If you want some kind of change you have to travel for a while at the speed of light. An astronaut who travels for ten years through the Milky Way at the speed of light will get a flipping surprise when he comes home. The earth has become a million years older.

Zombie Book 18/5

I think Dad drinks to escape from himself. But he wakes up every morning and is still among the cannibals.

Zombie Book 19/5

If I told Lisa Nordahl what it's like she'd be sad. If I told her exactly what it was like she'd definitely fall apart, start shaking there on the other side of the desk and POOF. So I don't.

Zombie Book 25/5

Tony came home today. That made me really happy. Everything felt the way it used to, for a while. I nagged him to box with me, but he didn't want to. I fetched the gloves and the egg timer. He thought I was soft in the head, wanting

154

to box, but he put on the gloves and knocked me down.

I got up and that made him angry and he hit me in the face. I fell down, everything spinning round, and he carried on hitting me. His main fuse must have blown. He sat astride me and punched and punched. I yelled at him to stop, but he hit me even though I was lying down.

When the egg timer rang he took off the gloves and left. He had been hitting me for ten minutes, even though I was on the floor. He made my nose bleed.

It hurts inside my head. Hurts all over my body. I ran into my room, scared, and Pi's cushion got blood on it. Tried to get it off with cold water but the blood only spread. Tony's crap.

Dad's asleep on the sofa. He's drunk. I'm never going to talk to Tony again. He can go to hell. Everyone can go to hell. Dick. Shag. Arsehole. What else is there? Breast. No, that's not the same kind of word. Gaydiarrhoeaprick.

Zombie Book 26/5

Parrot Earrings phoned today. She wanted to talk to Dad but I said he had a cold. She wondered how things were, and I said good. But she didn't believe me. She said she had arranged a family home for me in a safer environment. But I said I already had a family and a home. But Parrot Earrings went on and on and said the family home was in Bro and they had children of their own, and animals, horses and so on.

No, I said, I want to go to Lena, to Selet, if I have to go anywhere. Parrot Earrings said that was impossible; she said

I needed a secure, well-functioning family and that Lena didn't have the necessary qualifications. What did she mean, quali-fuck-ations, what's that when it's at home? What a crap word; I can hardly write it. I hung up. Parrot Earrings can go to hell. Who wants to live in a place called Bro?

Zombie Book 27/5

I've started making a weird noise that drives my teacher mad. I breathe in air through my nose and kind of make the roof of my mouth vibrate. Not the normal kind of sniffing sound – more like snoring. I can't stop making it. However hard I try, my brain keeps forcing me to do it. Miss sent me to the school nurse.

But when the school nurse wanted to hear it, I couldn't do it. She told me to take off my jumper because she wanted to listen to my lungs. And then she saw all the bruises and she went totally hysterical too. I should never have taken my jumper off.

Zombie Book 28/5

I opened a letter that came today. It was to my guardian. That was tricky. It took a while for me to work out what a guardian was. It's my dad.

The letter said: 'In accordance with the law on the care of young persons, Mik Backman will be placed without your consent in a more secure environment.'

There was also a load I didn't understand. The ninth

paragraph??? What??? What the hell is that??? Shit, who cares. The guardian is drunk and isn't going to get his hands on this letter. So that's no problem.

Zombie Book 2/6

Parrot Earrings and Gold Tooth came to school today. We had maths and sat calculating things. I was helping Ploppy with a sum when they suddenly walked into the classroom. Parrot Earrings said hello to the teacher. Gold Tooth stood by the door and I realised what they were going to do. They were going to capture me. I have actually thought about this, that the classroom is a trap because of the bars on the windows. But Ploppy and I have worked one of the locks loose.

Parrot Earrings told my teacher that I was to be collected in accordance with some law. Miss wondered what that law was, because she didn't want strangers just walking in and taking her pupils.

It was good my teacher argued with them. It gave me time to get to the window right at the back. It was easy to open and I jumped down into the bushes and ran.

Zombie Book 3/6

My dad's a car mechanic. My dad's a lawyer. My dad's a shoemaker. My dad's a baker. My dad's a lorry-driver. My dad's a dentist. My dad's a hairdresser. No, only joking. My dad's a spade. My dad's finished. I HATE HIM. EVERYONE CAN DIE.

Zombie Book 4/6

I sat in the library all day today. I've left school. It's not a secure environment for me.

I've been reading a book about whales. Forty million years ago there were whales with hind legs. The species was called Basilosaurus and it was a very big snake-like creature with massive jaws and big sharp canine teeth. It had no use for its hind legs. There was a picture of what it might have looked like. It reminded me of Snake Alone.

Zombie Book 6/6

I tried to tidy up today. Dad came home with clinking bags and said I was a good boy, and then he hid the bottles. He hides them so that I can't break them. He thinks I'm cruel and unfair to do that. Considering what a hard time he's had.

It looked nice at home. I hoovered all the rooms. Then he got drunk and wanted to die again. Said he only goes on living for my sake, for me and Tony.

I couldn't stand hearing it all again. I went down into the cellar. I've taken Pi's cushion down there. It's only now I realise how good it was at Lena's. I didn't think about it at the time. It's only when things aren't good that you realise how good it has been. You're too thick to realise things are good at the time. Only when Snake starts to move. A bit late.

There's so much I wish I'd said to Pi. I get a kind of ache when I think about it. So I try not to think of her.

Zombie Book 13/6

Parrot Earrings and Gold Tooth are standing outside the door. They've been ringing and ringing and ringing and ringing. They're standing there now as I'm writing this. And two policemen. First I hid under the bed with a torch, but they didn't stop ringing the bell. They talked through the letterbox and said I was going to get help. What shall I do? Tony isn't home and Dad's been gone two days.

I'm not going to open the door. I can stay here. I've got enough chocolate to survive. I looked in the wardrobe but the gun's gone. They're saying through the letterbox that they're going to break in. That I'm going to get help.

I've asked who decided that. They say they're the ones who make the decisions. I'll open the door if I can go to Lena. But they couldn't promise that because that wasn't their decision. So I'm not going to open it.

Then I said I'd jump from the balcony if they broke in. So it's deadlock. Another police car has pulled up outside. I went out and waved at them. The police officers waved back. Then I climbed around a bit on the outside of the balcony railing, but now I'm lying under the bed again.

The batteries in my torch are running out. There's only a faint yellow light. Parrot Earrings is talking through the letterbox and telling me I can go to Lena's as long as I give up that balcony nonsense and open the door. Now the batteries have run out.

PART 4

THE TORMENTORS

NEW PARENTS

Mik sat in the back seat. He looked out of the window and discovered it was already summer. He hadn't noticed. Green and lovely. Yellow dandelions and white fluffy clouds in a blue sky. A Swedish flag fluttered beside a red cottage. Summer? He was astonished.

He had said only two words during the entire journey.

'No.'

'Yes.'

No, he had said, when she asked if he was hungry. But she had given him a sandwich anyway.

Yes, he had said, when she asked if he would like the radio on. But then she changed her mind and thought it might just as well be quiet.

Now he was going to live with a family. He would have foster parents.

'A real functioning family,' Parrot Earrings had said.

They had promised him Lena. They had promised he would go to Selet.

'But you have to understand that wouldn't work,' Parrot Earrings had said. 'We have examined the case carefully and you have to understand this is the best thing for you.'

Parrot Earrings turned her head and looked at Mik in the back seat. She smiled: 'They've got a farm with animals. And a lovely lake with canoes and rowing boats. It'll be super.'

Mik pressed the cushion to the car window and leaned against it. It still had a smell of Pi, very faint but he could smell it. What was a functioning family? And what was it that functioned? Lena was his auntie and completely on her own. She functioned even though she was alone.

That's how he wanted it to be. When he grew up he would live all alone. Because then nothing weird or stupid would suddenly happen, unless you made it happen yourself. Like burn yourself on the cooker. Or trip over the mat, maybe, or fall off a chair. How brilliant it would be. Imagine coming home and being sure nothing had happened, because no one was at home. And nothing would happen unless you tripped over a mat or fell off a chair.

They turned into a driveway leading to a large yellow house with a garden and a flag pole in front. He saw the lake beyond with a little sandy beach and two canoes, one red and one blue. To the right of the yellow house was a large stable block where a girl was leading a horse, and on the left was a long, low building with big fenced enclosures. An enormous black dog hurled itself against the wire and barked at the car.

Mik recoiled, absolutely terrified.

'What's that?'

'Didn't I tell you? They breed dogs too and run a boarding kennel.'

Parrot Earrings looked up at him in the rear-view mirror.

'That'll be fun, won't it? Lots of dogs. And there's the stables with horses. I'm sure you'll be able to ride, too. Perfect paradise.'

On the gravel drive in front of the yellow house stood a boy holding an air rifle. Just behind him a bare-chested man was mowing the lawn between the apple trees, or maybe they were pear trees. Parrot Earrings parked in front of the house. The man switched off the lawnmower and called out, 'Hello, welcome.'

The lawnmower man was suntanned and had big muscles, which scared Mik. He looked as if he was hard and cruel. The dogs barked. The boy with the air rifle said nothing. He had red hair and freckles and looked like a nerd. A nasty nerd.

He grinned at Mik, loaded the gun and shot at a tin can. The door of the house opened and a dark-haired woman came out, smiling.

'Welcome. Coffee and buns are served in the kitchen. And juice for the children.'

162

'Oh, that'll be lovely,' said Parrot Earrings.

'Or shall we sit outside? It's such nice weather.'

'No, no,' said Parrot Earrings. 'The kitchen will be absolutely fine.'

She followed the dark-haired woman through the door. The man had collected his shirt, which was hanging in an apple tree, or pear tree, or whatever it was.

The boy broke open the air rifle, loaded it, aimed up into a tree and fired. A bird flapped and fell to the ground, circled its wings for a moment and then went quite still.

'Good shot, Niklas,' said the man as he buttoned his shirt.

The boy examined the bird, holding it up by one leg. It was quite a big bird. Its wings hung outstretched and blood dripped past its eye and down its beak.

'A thrush.'

'It's dead,' said Mik.

'Course it is. I shot it.'

'Why?'

'Why not?'

'Don't argue about it,' said the man. 'They eat up the cherries later in summer and crap everywhere.'

The plate of cinnamon buns was enormous.

'Come on, help yourselves.'

Mik hesitated.

'Well, go on,' said Parrot Earrings. 'Don't be shy.'

He took a bun.

'We must introduce ourselves,' said the dark-haired woman with the plate of buns. 'My name is Eva and this is our son Niklas.'

'And I'm Niklas's dad and my name is Rickard. We have horses and dogs and two goats.'

Mik was given juice and took another bun. The door slammed. A girl came in and sat down at the kitchen table.

'This is Louise, our sixteen-year-old, who –'

'Give it a rest,' said Louise.

The girl took a bun and glared at Mik. She was blonde with crystal-clear blue eyes and Mik stopped chewing. She was so beautiful, or attractive, or pretty – no, not pretty, something else. So attractive you couldn't describe it. So attractive that when you looked away or closed your eyes you couldn't remember. The memory sort of didn't last.

'What are you gawking at?'

She was wearing a thin, light-coloured blouse and her nipples protruded through the material. He became dizzy and afraid, looked down at his bun and couldn't work out what was going on.

'This is Mik,' said Parrot Earrings, patting Mik's head. 'And the plan is for him to live here with you.'

'Right,' said Louise. 'Just as long as I don't have to see him.'

She took two buns, stood up and left the table.

The mum, who was called Eva, nodded her head in a weird way and pulled a face.

'Hormones. More coffee?'

'Yes, please,' said Parrot Earrings. 'What a lovely home you have! I mean, this is really how it should be. This is how we ought to live. Not in a flat in town.'

'Yes, well, it comes at a price,' said the dad, whose name was Rickard. 'Sometimes you can get tired of this too.'

'What do you mean?' said the mum.

'What do I mean? Oh, nothing.'

Parrot Earrings chatted about the practical details with Eva and Rickard. They flicked through some papers, slurped their coffee.

'Well, there we are,' said Parrot Earrings. 'I'd better be off if I'm going to get back to Solna before I finish for the day, otherwise it'll be overtime.'

She stood up.

'Thank you and I hope everything works out. Otherwise I'm here to help.'

'Not a problem,' said Rickard, holding out a huge fist.

They shook hands and Parrot Earrings headed for the door, stopped and turned around.

'Oh, yes, was there anything you can think of, Mik? Or is everything okay?'

'Okay,' he said, and she smiled.

'Everything will be fine, you'll see,' said Parrot Earrings.

She waved at the kitchen window from outside, got into the car, started it and drove off.

Mik reached out for another bun.

'Oh, no you don't,' said Eva. 'You've had enough now.'

She put the plate of buns away.

～～

The room that was to be his was in the basement and had narrow windows high up under the ceiling. The walls were covered in forest-patterned wallpaper. Fir trees, an endless row of fir trees.

'What have you got there?' asked Eva, nodding towards his arm.

Mik looked down at his cushion.

'My cushion.'

'Comfort cushion, is it?'

Eva took the cushion and continued, 'Only little children have things like that, don't they? I'll look after it.'

And so she left, with the words, 'Make yourself at home.'

Mik opened his bag. He had three pairs of trousers, two jumpers, four pairs of socks, five pairs of underpants, five T-shirts, a belt, a toothbrush, toothpaste, his mobile, the knife and his front door keys. He put the knife in the belt. He folded the clothes and put them in the chest of drawers. He hid the keys under the jumpers, changed his mind and shoved them in his pocket.

He made the bed with the sheet, duvet cover and pillow cases that had been put out for him, and when he was finished he sat on the bed and stared at the forest wallpaper. He had a strong feeling that no one here would think he was funny.

~~~

Rickard and Niklas came into the room.

'So, here you are,' said Rickard. 'Your own room and everything; that's good. Just a couple of things. We all have to lend a hand here. No one can get out of it, otherwise it won't work. And we have rules, but Niklas can run through those with you later. We've got fourteen dogs of our own and five in the boarding kennels. It's a lot of work and we thought it would be a very good idea if you helped Niklas with the dogs. You can give them food and then muck out the runs and keep the dog kennels clean.

'Dog poo,' said Niklas, grinning.

'You can go down straight away and say hello to the dogs.'

LOCKED IN WITH A POTTY

There were about ten dog runs with rusty wire netting outside the dog kennels. It looked like a concentration camp. It smelled of dog shit and dog piss.

Two large dark dogs growled softly behind the bars and barked. Others kept quiet and roamed backwards and forwards behind the fencing. Most of the runs appeared to be empty.

'The others are in the kennels,' said Niklas. 'They're out here during the day and we take them in at night. They have their own enclosures so they don't tear each other to pieces. We've mostly got Riesenschnauzers.'

Riesenschnauzers. Mik shuddered.

Niklas grinned. 'The biggest ones, old Jasack and Bass, weigh over fifty kilos and are seventy centimetres high. Sack and Bass can't stand Qvint and Rip. They must never be let out at the same time or be in the same run. Otherwise they'll kill each other. Nian and Narp can't be together either. Are you listening?'

'Yes,' said Mik.

He was listening, and he realised he had arrived in hell.

Niklas went on, 'Jasack is the oldest and biggest and the king. But he's old and has only got four teeth left and his breath stinks. He only likes Dad and tries to bite everyone else.'

Niklas looked at Mik with a superior expression. Mik knew Niklas was the bullying kind. They were easy to recognise: if you went down to the street to show everyone what a lovely big toad you'd found, there was always one boy who wanted to know what colour it was underneath. But there was also always the boy who wanted to know what a toad would look like after a flight down from the tenth floor.

Mik knew he was the toad. Foster child and Niklas's toad.

And why did these people have dogs? Wasn't it bad enough as it was?

'Come on, I'll teach you the dog duties,' said Niklas, opening the door to the kennels.

They entered a large room with steel workbenches along the walls. Stainless steel bowls were piled up high. There was a grimy bathtub and a shower hose. On the walls hung leads, muzzles, combs and brush-type things. There were two big blue plastic barrels full of dog food.

The whole room smelled of dog food and stale dog. And behind it lingered the stink of piss and shit. At the end of the room was a long passage with cage doors on either side.

'This is the workroom where the food is prepared and the dogs are groomed. You must never have more than one dog in here at a time. In the other section are the enclosures.'

Niklas chatted on about what you should and shouldn't do. Which food some dogs must have and others mustn't. Mik looked at the muzzles and leads and all these shiny chains. Chains, chains and more chains.

'Those are the choke chains,' said Niklas. 'For the big ones, to stop them doing what they want.'

Niklas pointed to a piece of paper taped to the wall, listing how much each dog should have of what. It was an endless list of dog names and types of food.

'Jasack has to have his heart medication every day. You mix it in with his food. It's that tin there.'

He turned around and looked at Mik.

'Are you getting all this or what?'

'Yeah, I get it.'

'You'd better not make any mistakes or I'll get the blame and then Rickard will go mental. Jasack is his favourite dog so he has to have the best food and be looked after well.'

Niklas lined up some bowls, scooped dry food into each and mixed it with water.

'Bring the bowls and follow me,' said Niklas, and he walked into the passage with the cages.

Mik stayed where he was in the opening. It resembled a cellar passageway with fenced-off storage areas on each side. The difference was that here there was a black monster behind each door.

'I don't do dogs,' said Mik.

'What do you mean? Are you allergic or something?'

'No, I'm scared.'

Niklas smiled and the freckles on his face lengthened into narrow strips.

'They don't all bite.'

170

'How do you know which is which, when they all look the same?'

'They don't all look the same. You'll learn. You only have to feed them morning and evening. And there's always one who's crapped in his kennel during the night. Then you've got to scrub it clean.'

'Are the doors properly closed?'

'Yes. Come on, get going.'

Mik walked down the passage, his eyes moving anxiously from one dog to the next. They glared back, watchful. One gave a low snarl and the others joined in. They could smell his fear, and then all hell broke loose. Dogs threw themselves against the wire netting, barking. The netting rattled and bulged. The dogs tore round like black demons. Completely mental.

He saw eyes – black eyes and white inner eyelids. Glistening teeth in red, warty gums. Warm breath smelling of their stomachs. Dog spit sprayed in his face. Mik dropped the bowls but stayed rooted to the spot. The fierce barking went through his body like electric shocks. Jaws snapped. Teeth twisted the wire netting. Dogs on hind legs, bigger than he was. Black, with massive white teeth. They hated him, they wanted to kill him and his body wouldn't obey him.

He closed his eyes, put his hands to his ears, bent forwards and pressed his palms together tight, tight. Swayed, sobbed.

Something warm in his trousers. It ran down his legs and turned cold.

He had wet himself.

~~~

Mik sat on his bed and stared into the forest wallpaper. Never had he felt so lost. Tengil's men patrolled the ramparts with sword and spear. He would never get away from here alive. He felt the blood stop flowing in his veins. Felt his heart stiffen and stop beating. He was already dead. Nothing else was possible.

Eva stood in the door.

'You don't wet your bed as well?' she said.

'No.'

'Good. Now go to bed and I'll lock the door. There's a potty under the bed.'

So she went, and he was locked in with a potty.

He wanted his cushion.

He wanted to go home.

All he wanted to do was get up out of bed and go home.

But which direction was it?

And the door was locked. Why had she locked it? Mik fingered his dead mobile. He wanted to phone Pi. He wanted to phone Tony and Lena. He wanted to phone someone who would save him. He wanted to phone Tengil and tell him to go to hell. Mik let out a cry and hurled the mobile at the wall so it made a groove in the forest wallpaper and a mess of the phone. He placed a chair against the wall, climbed up and felt the window. It was nailed shut. Far down below was the lake.

The evening sky was golden yellow and the water still and shimmering. Someone was swimming with a horse at the little beach. Mik saw a bird sitting high up in a tree. He knew nothing about birds, but he recognised this one. It was a hawk owl.

THE DOG FEEDER

The dogs barked and stood on their hind legs behind the wire fencing. Mik wiped the dog saliva from his face, pressed his hand to his bladder and convinced himself there was not a drop left. He had peed several times before going to the dog kennels. But how was he going to get the food bowls into the cages without opening the doors? And what if he needed a crap? Suppose he messed his pants? That simply mustn't happen. If it did he might as well let himself be eaten alive.

Oh shit, his whole body was shaking. His front teeth chattered. The sound of the barking was tearing his ears to shreds.

If you refuse, Niklas had said, I'll shoot you with the air rifle. A rogue shot in the eye. How unfortunate that would be.

Could they really tell the difference between him and the food? What would be left? Perhaps a piece of bone, chewed clean. Probably not even that. They crushed the bones to get at the marrowbone jelly. Marrowbone jelly contained a lot of goodness. It was nutritious.

If he died, who would care? Because there was no doubt he was going to die. He had mixed together fourteen bowls of food. He had to open fourteen cages. How great were his chances of surviving? Fairly small, and this was day one of … ? How long did he have to be here? The dogs barked; the wire mesh rattled. He might just as well die right away. Shit himself and die. They probably ate shit too.

Mik opened the cage door. The dog fell silent and stopped hurling itself at the wire mesh. Throat, thought Mik, protect your throat. But the dog didn't throw itself at him. It ran round in tight circles and whined until the bowl stood on the concrete floor. The dog gulped down the food, swallowing without chewing, and when the food had gone it lay on its bed in the cage, completely quiet and with its chin resting on its paws. Mik quickly picked up the bowl and closed the cage door.

The next dog behaved the same way, and the one after that. They only cared about the food, not him. They fell silent, one by one.

In the ninth cage something odd happened. This dog was slightly smaller than the others and didn't come rushing up to the food bowl. It cowered in a corner of the cage, trembling. Number Nine was afraid of him. It didn't dare eat while Mik was in the cage. He had to go out and shut the door before the dog would come up to the bowl.

The big dog, Jasack, had his food last. His coat was matted and resembled a wilted bramble bush. The massive head looked like a tyrannosaurus with bad teeth. He ate slowly and farted. The bowl got so clean it gleamed. His legs were stiff and he lay down with great difficulty. Jasack farted again. Apart from that, it was silent in the kennels.

Mik looked into Number Nine's cage. The dog backed away.

'Boo,' said Mik.

Number Nine jumped.

'Only joking.'

~~~

Hello Tony,

Everything smells of dog shit. Seven days. It feels like seven years. It's evening and I'm sitting locked in my room. I'm a prisoner here. A concentration camp. It's a room in the cellar with forest wallpaper. Tall pines from floor to ceiling. When I wake up in the morning I think I'm lost in a forest. This is a strange place I've ended up in. We have porridge for breakfast. You know how I hate porridge. It's all going to go horribly wrong. But I think it already has. My dysfunctional foster brother is called Niklas and when he's not giving me grief or shooting birds he's on the internet checking out gun sites. My dysfunctional foster sister is called Louise and whips her horse. My dysfunctional foster father is called Rickard. He's always in a foul mood and finding more work for me to do. I rake the gravel, cut the grass, feed the dogs. In the beginning I was afraid the dogs would kill me. But they're stupid and only think of food. My dysfunctional foster mother is angry. If I eat too much she has a go at me. If I don't eat enough she says I'm so spoiled the food isn't good enough for me. I get totally nervous and don't know how to behave. She cries when no one is looking. I wonder if Niklas knows why he shoots birds. If Louise knows why she whips her horse. If their mum knows why she cries. It's important to know why. You can't throw a stone at someone's head without knowing why. I know why I'm here. I wonder if Dad does.

I'm locked in with a potty. Good night.

Best wishes,

Mik.

THE DOG TURD KING

It was quiet at the breakfast table. Mik looked down into his bowl of porridge. Slimy lumps of glue swam in the milk. He didn't like porridge, never had. If he held his nose it didn't taste so bad. But it wasn't the taste that was disgusting, it was the slimy feeling of swallowing a fistful of frogspawn. And holding his nose didn't help. He was going to be sick.

'What are you up to?' said Rickard. 'Eat like a normal human being. You can't sit here making a fuss every morning.'

Louise glared at him. 'Is that object going to live here long?'

'Where else would he live?' said Eva.

Niklas didn't have to eat porridge. He ate cornflakes. Mik had tried to get cornflakes too. He wasn't allowed. Here the rule was to eat porridge for breakfast. Unprocessed oats to provide the energy to cope with real work. When he tried to ask why Niklas didn't have to eat porridge, Rickard flew into a rage.

'Stop questioning every damn thing. You live here now and you'll just have to follow our rules.'

'I'm going to be sick,' said Mik.

'Don't be disgusting at the table,' said Eva.

Nobody believed him. But if he was sick now, all over the table, would he be given cornflakes? Why not? Actually there were so many weird rules here that it was completely impossible to know when you were breaking one.

The tadpoles wanted to come up. They wriggled in his throat. Mik tried to think of something else. He thought of the lake down there and of the red canoe. And then for a while of the blue canoe. Which one was best?

'Can I paddle one of the canoes?' he asked and swallowed.

'Can you swim?'

'Yes.'

'Are you going to paddle home, then?' said Louise and laughed.

Mik looked at her breasts. He felt the contents of his stomach rising. The tadpoles were swimming round, going faster and faster in a whirlpool. He held his gaze a little too long on the breasts. It wasn't deliberate. He swallowed and swallowed.

'Filthy little kid!' shouted Louise, standing up. 'He really annoys me.'

Eva looked at Mik in astonishment.

'What has he done?'

Mik swallowed. His throat stung from all the oxygen.

'He's always staring at my breasts. He's disturbed.'

'Yep,' said Niklas. 'That's why he's here.'

Mik was sick in his porridge bowl. His stomach threw up cascades, wave after wave until it was empty. Louise screamed and rushed from the table. Niklas stared wide-eyed and noticed he had porridge in his cornflakes.

'What on earth ...' shouted Eva.

All the porridge was back on the table. Tears ran from Mik's eyes. He stopped breathing, got tunnel vision and fainted face down in his bowl. Rickard lifted up his head by the hair and held it there until he came round.

'Can I have cornflakes instead?'

~~~

Yes, porridge is disgusting, thought Mik, as he walked towards the dog kennels. On a scale of one to ten it was a six, maybe a seven. It all depended what you compared it with. Sick is disgusting. Blood is disgusting. Death is not disgusting. Snakes are not disgusting. Spiders are not disgusting. You mustn't confuse things you are afraid of with things that are disgusting. Mix things up and you won't know where you are.

There were dog turds in every cage.

Rickard had left it too late before taking the dogs out of their cages. Turds in every cage hadn't happened before. The disgusting thing about dog poo was that it was so like human poo. Horse poo, elk poo and rabbit poo were something completely different and not at all disgusting. You could have them in your pocket. But dog poo. You wouldn't want that in your pocket.

The stench hung so heavy and brown over the entire dog kennels that it ought to be visible. Mik filled a bucket with hot water and threw in a few capfuls of cleaning liquid with a lemon fragrance. First he picked up what was possible to pick up using a spade and scraper and put it in the wheelbarrow, cage by cage. Then he cleaned with a mop and cloth, but the lemon didn't stand a chance. The combination resulted in a smell that was completely sick. Lemon poo.

Perhaps a slightly more yellow smell, but the brown won hands down.

Dog poo wasn't simply dog poo. Some turds were hard and neat and easy to get up with the spade. Easy work with not a splodge left to mess up the concrete floor. They were dream turds from dogs that were healthy. From these dream turds there was a whole scale of softer varieties down to a watery brown muck. Those dogs were not too healthy. In the cages of Number Nine and Jasack, the poo was always hopelessly runny. Cleaning cloth, lemon liquid and effort. Giving the dogs their food was a minor thing compared with cleaning up their poo.

Every time he finished he ran down to the beach, but the smell hung around. It had crawled into his body. It was impossible to get rid of it. The shit was under his nails. The shit went in through his pores. The shit was mixed in with his blood. He had a faint but constant taste of dog shit far back on his tongue. Dog shit and a little lemon.

Mik wrung the cloth out over the bucket. The difficult thing was cleaning it up without spreading it around. A technique was required, otherwise he would soon have smeared it over the whole floor of the cage.

To cope with the work you had to think of it as a kind of paint or a bad pea soup and not think that it had been moulded into curves on its way through the intestines of these vile creatures and squeezed out through a bumhole.

The best thing was to think about something completely different: wonder what Pi's doing now? Perhaps she's swimming in Lake Selet? Wonder what it looks like there in the summer? Maybe she's swimming naked? He couldn't picture that and was bewildered that he had even thought of it.

Mik cleaned the cloth and the mop and rinsed out the bucket. He pushed the wheelbarrow outside and emptied it on the dung heap behind the hen house. Now there were twenty-four hours until he had to scrub dog poo again. Filled with a sense of freedom, he ran down to the lake. Took deep breaths, airing his lungs.

Louise came riding up from the beach. Instantly Mik stopped. She held the horse motionless in front of him. It was big. Shiny, wet, black and big. Louise sat high up, luminous in a wet white strappy top.

The horse stamped and snorted. Its hooves were huge and very close. Mik backed away. She stared at him and, pointing her whip out sideways, said, 'Go drown yourself.'

He stepped down into the ditch and she rode past.

The sun was high over the lake and the water lay as shiny as melted metal. Some ducks came out from the reeds and flew outstretched over the lake with whining wing beats. He pushed the canoe out into the water and stepped in carefully. Silently he glided out. Small fish leapt on the surface. Screams and laughter from children swimming could be heard in the distance. Mik held the paddle over his knees. It dripped cold water onto his leg. The canoe glided along and he held his open hand in the water. It was cool.

Somewhere there is a pretty little stream with a stone bridge, just like in Nangijala. That's where I'll sit and wait for Tony. Perhaps ten years, perhaps thirty, but for me it will be like a single breath. And when he comes we'll go fishing in the stream together. Petals from the cherry trees fall like snow on us. They stick in our hair and he laughs. I'll wait for Tony and we'll go fishing.

She is standing there with her green umbrella by the house and Tony says, 'Are we going to live here?'

'Yes, it's our house.'

And she has made pancakes.

How far is it to Nangijala?

He was already a long way from the shore. Out here he was free. He lay down in the canoe, looking up at the summer sky. One cloud looked like a duck. Another one looked like a bear, then came a dragon, followed by a bus.

Wonder what kind of fish there are in this stream?

At ten past nine he was locked in his room. He had fallen asleep in the canoe and drifted a long way away. A wind had come up and it had taken him the whole day to paddle back against the headwind. He had blisters on his hands. Rickard and Eva were absolutely furious. That was the last time he would be paddling a canoe.

~~

Hello Tony,

I've thought a lot about dog poo. I mean, I'm not trying to be funny. This isn't poo and fart jokes. Dog poo isn't funny. What I was thinking was that I'm not afraid of dog poo. I can hold it in my hands. I can switch off the poo section in my brain. But I'm afraid I'm going mad. If you can pick up dog poo with your hands then your actual main socket in your brain must be loose. Think if I suddenly start eating dog turds? I don't think I can stay here. I'm so homesick. A hawk owl sits in the tree down by the lake. That means something. If anything means anything. But I think it does.

I still haven't had a letter from you. Don't you have a pen, or what?

Best wishes,
The Dog Turd King.

DID MICHAEL ROCKEFELLER PEE IN HIS TROUSERS?

All the dogs had been given their food. It was quiet in the kennels. The strange thing was that the dogs didn't all look the same any longer. At first Mik had only seen big black hairy dogs, but now he could tell the difference between them. They also had their different ways, just like people. Some were disobedient; some seemed intelligent, others incredibly thick. Number Nine was afraid; Jasack was old, whiny and farty. And all of them were desperately hungry. They lived for mealtimes, and the person who fed them became their friend; it was as simple as that. In fact, the dogs were the most normal things here. They ate and crapped and wanted to play and run.

Mik collected the bowls and started washing them up. Niklas came into the workroom.

'Hi. Do you want to do something cool?'

Mik stood amazed, the frothy washing-up brush in his hand.

'What kind of something cool?'

'All you've got to do is hold this can.'

'What for?'

'You've just got to stand there and hold the can. It's not difficult.'

'And what are you going to do?'

'Shoot.'

'The can?'

'Yes.'

'Never,' said Mik and turned away to carry on with the washing-up.

'Are you scared? I can hit anything. I'm a good shot.'

'You can just as easily put the can on a rock or a tree stump,' said Mik, piling the bowls on the draining rack.

Niklas grinned; Mik knew that, even though he had his back to him. You could hear it because his smile wasn't silent. It gave off a smearing sound. Maybe it was the freckles protesting about being pulled into lines in his ugly mug.

'You're scared. You'll wet yourself.'

'No, I won't, because I'm not going to hold your rotten can. Stand it on a rock.'

'That's not as exciting.'

'Then you can hold the can and I'll shoot,' said Mik.

'You can't shoot. And if you don't hold the can I'll tell Louise you spy on her when she's swimming.'

'I've never done that,' said Mik.

'She swims naked. Her and the horse.'

'I haven't watched.'

'Doesn't matter. She'll kill you when she finds out.'

Mik put the last food bowl on the draining rack. Now he

was Niklas's toad again. Up to the tenth floor, freefall and see what happens. Two days earlier, when Mik was sweaty from cutting the grass outside the kennels, Niklas had kindly brought him a glass of water. It was vinegar. It was a surprise.

This time there was at least a choice. Be trampled to death by Louise and her big black horse or hold the can. A third choice would have been to knock Niklas down. Only head-butt him, smack that idiotic grin so it turned into a mess of blood and teeth between fat swollen lips.

But on a scale of one to ten the chances were zero that he would get away with it. Hell, thought Mik. I might be able to put up with being in this awful place if I could only be left in peace. If I did my work and then could be left alone. Dogs, dog poo, potty, porridge and forest wallpaper. But being a toad …

'I never miss,' said Niklas. 'This morning I shot a wagtail at thirty metres. And that's a very small bird. It'll be okay, as long as you hold your big ears in.'

Mik stood in front of a large oak tree and held the can as far away from his body as possible. He tried to make his arm grow, stretched it so the tendons clicked.

'Good,' said Niklas and walked ten long paces away.

He broke open the rifle, loaded it, lifted and aimed. Mik stared at the rifle barrel and felt sweat attacks pump through his skin. His knees shook. Niklas lowered the gun.

'It's too close. Too easy.'

He took another ten long paces. Lifted the rifle and aimed.

Mik tilted his head back and looked up into the leafy branches of the oak tree. The shaking spread from his legs up into his whole body.

'You have to look at me, not up in the tree.'

Mik thought Niklas aimed directly at his face. His throat tightened. There was a rushing in his head. Did he need to pee? No, he mustn't need to pee. Rather a bullet in the face than pee his pants. Niklas lowered the rifle and took another five paces.

'From this distance,' yelled Niklas, 'you have to aim a little higher. A bit above. Really you should have the can on your head. That would be exciting.'

Mik had stopped breathing. His field of vision shrank. At first everything took on a pale green colour, which then shifted to red. It was as if he had zoomed in on the rifle barrel. The rushing in his head grew to a scream. His pulse felt like pressure waves through his body. The can weighed a ton in his hand. He was going to be blown up.

'Stand still,' shouted Niklas.

My eye, thought Mik. He's going to hit me in the eye. The shot rang out and he collapsed in a heap.

~~~

The sun filtered down through the leaves of the oak tree. Green transparent leaves rustled in the wind. Mik lay spread-eagled on the ground. He filled his lungs with air. Shut one eye – it worked. Shut the other one – that worked too. But something worse had happened. His trousers were wet. Niklas leaned over him, holding the can.

'Look. Bullseye. But you've peed your pants.'

And off he went with his rifle.

～～～

Hi Tony,

Scientist Michael Rockefeller from New York was on an exploration trip to New Guinea. He fell in the water, swam ten kilometres and dragged himself ashore where there were cannibals. Since then no one has seen him. I feel like Michael Rockefeller, except I can't swim and the people here aren't cannibals. Yesterday I made a poster for my room, which said Dog Turd King, but Rickard took it down. But no one can take away the dog-shit smell. Obviously you can't have that kind of poster in a functional family. What it is exactly that functions, I'm not sure. While I've been living here I've thought a lot about Mum. I've started to remember what she looked like. I can even hear her voice in my head. I usually think about when we went to the funfair. I can't tell the difference any more between what I've made up and what really happened. Sometimes I feel as if I don't even exist - that I've only made it up. Perhaps nothing exists. Wonder if Michael Rockefeller peed in his pants when he saw the cannibals?

Best wishes,

Dog Turd King.

THE BLUE TRAIN

The smell of dog turds didn't bother him. They smelled, of course, but it wasn't revolting. It should have been. Mik thought he might just as well have been lying on the floor scraping up spilled yoghurt. But brown yoghurt. Perhaps you could get used to everything? Mik stopped mopping suddenly. Looked at the brown muck.

Used to everything?

Had he become brainwashed? Like a prisoner of war in a concentration camp? Was he broken? Was he finished? Did he agree to everything? Had the Tormentors broken him?

Mik sat on the floor, leaned his back against the wire mesh and looked up at the ceiling and a bare light bulb. He thought, Mock execution with an air rifle.

Locked in with a potty.

Dog muck and disgusting food.

Was all this planned? Was he to be broken and become a dribbling retard? Was that the plan?

But whose plan? And why?

It wasn't good to think. Everything suddenly seemed much worse than it had been. He ought to write a letter and protest. He ought to write to … well, who? Parrot Earrings? The Paragraph? Tengil?

~~~

He finished cleaning the kennels and ran down to the lake to swim. He pushed out the canoe, even though it was forbidden, and paddled far out. It was hot; had to be the hottest day of the summer. The sun beat down and the air quivered over the surface of the water. From the shore came wild laughter and happy shrieks as children dived from jetties and boats. Some were playing with an inflatable mattress, others with a big red and white beach ball. Mik stopped paddling, lay down in the canoe and looked up at the sky.

Imagine he was Skorpan Lionheart but hadn't ended up in Nangijala. He was Skorpan who had ended up right in the middle of hell. He probably died there in the swimming pool, and somehow it had all gone wrong. For some, for a very small percentage, it went wrong. And where had Tony ended up? He never answered any letters. Perhaps they couldn't reach him where he was?

Only the white doves of Nangijala could fly across all skies with their messages, as far as they liked. From Cherry Valley and into the whole universe. But did it have to be a dove? And did it have to be white? The pigeons in Solna shopping centre were grey and scabby. Or would any bird do? And how far did the bird have to fly? How far was it to Tony? It could be an incredibly long way. What if I'm already dead? thought Mik. If I'm already dead in death. And dead in the death of deaths. Nangijala to Nangilima, to … where am I, exactly? And why has Tengil got to all the places first?

~~~

Mik paddled back and pulled the canoe up onto the shore. He turned it upside down so that it wouldn't fill with water if it rained. A horse snorted and he could hear the sound of hooves. Louise came riding down to the beach. Mik hid under the canoe. She didn't see him. The horse was allowed to graze freely while she took off all her clothes. Stark naked, she walked out into the water. Mik saw it all clearly and held his breath. He was afraid, wanted to get away. He crawled out to run off.

The canoe flipped over and hit the pebbles. Louise turned round and screamed. She ran frantically out of the water. Mik ran, but she was wild with anger and ran fast, lashing at him with her riding whip. She struck his neck, and a fierce, stinging blow brought him to his knees. Then lash after lash rained down. He crawled and she whipped.

'Stop,' he whimpered. 'Stop.'

But she didn't stop. Completely naked and with a hysterical look in her eyes she raised the whip again and again.

'You filthy little beast,' she said. 'Look, then, if you really want to. You dirty little creep. You're all the same.'

She started to cry. She stopped whipping him and cried with her hands in front of her face. Mik got up and walked directly into the forest.

He walked a long way, continuing until he could no longer see the lake. Came to a road but didn't follow it, keeping instead to the forest. Stumbled over roots, stumps and branches. He walked like a robot, automatically. His legs took one step, and one more, and one more, without knowing where he was heading.

In the distance he heard barking. It was coming from the kennels. He recognised the dogs' barks. The muffled one was Bas. Number Nine's was screeching, sharp. His entire body hurt. His arms were striped red. The skin on one shoulder was broken and bleeding. Someone else would have to clear up the dog shit now. He'd had enough.

The forest got denser and the undergrowth thicker. Then he came into an area of newly planted trees with thin, cruel branches that snagged and tore. He struggled through it only to emerge into endless bare ground where the trees had been felled and there were only stumps and brambles. Bloody hell.

The sweat ran and the sun's rays burned him. He climbed up a slope, chased by horseflies and midges. His stomach ached with hunger and he started thinking of food. Sausages, pancakes, pizza. Hamburgers.

Mik came out onto a railway line, high up and with double tracks. It was on a long, slow bend. The rails shone in the sunlight. The electric rails hummed. There was a smell of electricity, a dry hint of burning. He took off his white T-shirt which was streaked with pine resin and dirt, and stuffed it securely into the waistband of his trousers. The sweat was running in rivers, the whip marks stung, and he was

193

incredibly thirsty. If you're going to run away you should have food and water with you.

He looked along the track, first in one direction, then the other. Which way should he go? Did it matter? Best to walk away from the sun so as not to be blinded by the rails.

Mik tried walking on the sleepers. They were nice and even but the distance between them made them impossible to walk on. It made his steps look ridiculous. Stiff and clumsy. He couldn't get into any kind of rhythm. He walked alongside them for a while but the chippings were so coarse and rough he twisted his ankle. The sleepers were better, but nothing was good. He tried balancing on the rail with his arms held out. That went better.

There was no shade on the railway line and the heat of the sun worked its way under the skin on his head and barbecued his brain. And that made him start thinking of barbecued chicken. No, he mustn't think of food now. He must get away, far away, before they put the bloodhounds on his trail.

Mik wound his T-shirt around his head like a turban to protect it from the sun. Hungry but free. It was over now. No one would tell him what to do ever again.

Mik stood still with his arms outstretched. There was an odd feeling under the soles of his feet: small, tickling vibrations. They grew bigger and made his legs shake all the way up to his knees. The rails were alive.

Train.

A metallic noise. It came from behind but he couldn't see it yet on the long, gradual bend. He remained standing on the rails, swaying, balancing.

Was it a big train? A long one? Fast?

The rails vibrated furiously under his feet. A monster tearing towards him. I must jump down now; I must. Wild terror flooded through him and his joints locked. His brain melted into a gluey mess and his thoughts were drawn out in long, sinewy threads.

How close is close?

The train appeared round the bend at a terrifying speed. It was absolutely shocking. Mik saw it against the sunlight, a dark monster with three lights for eyes. The vibrations travelled up to his head. He shook. His thigh muscles quivered. Mik felt his saliva turn electric and sour and thicken to long strings inside his mouth. He was paralysed, frozen in glass. The sound of metal wheel against metal rail rushed towards him, and blasting through the entire universe was the sound of a horn.

The air shattered into a thousand pieces.

Mik hurled himself off the track. The train tore past. He crept into a ball, covering his face with his arms. He was slammed by the backdraught. Wheels turned. Metal ground and shook against metal. Dust whirled through the air.

That was close, all right.

The train leaned into the curve and disappeared. He recognised it. The local train. The usual blue local train.

Mik followed the railway track out of the forest. First he came across a few small houses and a level crossing. Soon blocks of flats were shooting up above the trees. He came to a station, climbed up onto the platform and waited for the blue train home.

THE CHOCOLATE
WAFER THIEF

The tobacconist's was no longer there. All that was left in the window was a small pile of sawdust. Mik tried the door. It was locked and there was a notice behind the glass: 'Shop closed down. Premises to rent', followed by a telephone number.

From the pizzeria came an aroma that made his stomach turn over. He had no money. Perhaps there was some at home? Money for a calzone. Cheese, ham and mushrooms. Tony had money; he was sure to be home. Mik stood for a while outside the entrance to the flats. Breathed in the air through his nostrils. The smell of home. A mixture of cat piss, bricks, mortar and something indefinably stale coming up from the cellar. Quickly he ran up the stairs and put his front door key in the lock.

It didn't fit. He went through the keys on his key ring – yes, it was the right key, but it didn't fit, even though it was his own front door. It had the dent from the hockey puck they had knocked about in the stairwell. And the groove Tony had made with his knife to the left of the letterbox. Everything was as it should be. He would have recognised this door out of a thousand doors. Mik tugged at the door handle and rang the bell. Silence.

Why didn't his key fit? He went through his bunch of keys again. It was the right one, no doubt about that. He knew exactly what the notches on his front door key looked like. He tried again. Then he understood. It was the wrong lock. The right key but the wrong lock.

The name plate was new. There was a different name on the door: H. Stål. Who the hell was H. Stål?

Mik wandered aimlessly around Solna shopping centre. He tried to see if anyone was home at Ploppy's, but no one answered even though he rang ten times.

The car showroom was finished. He went in and looked at shiny new cars until he was told to leave. Tried again to see if Ploppy was at home, but nobody came to the door.

Everything looked the same as usual. There was Råsunda Road, with the buses coming and going. Everything seemed the same. Except it wasn't. Everything was something else entirely.

He didn't know how long he had been wandering around. His brain wasn't working. His legs and body took on a life of their own and took him to the museum. The elephant skeleton was still there, with its empty eye sockets. The stuffed tiger hadn't moved a single millimetre.

Mik went up the staircase and out onto the bridge above the whale skeletons. Yellow vertebrae, dry ribs, cracked skulls. The room smelled of old death. It felt good. This was exactly what he looked like inside. Someone had tried to wipe the graffiti off the biggest skull, but it had only made a mess and you could still read the word 'shag'.

Mik pressed the whale sound button and listened to the mournful signals. Thought about Lena, Selet and Pi. Pressed it over and over again until he started to cry.

Someone put a hand on his shoulder.

'We're closing soon.'

Mik turned around with tears streaming down his face. It was the security guard.

'Have you paid your entrance fee?'

'No, but I'm going now. I'm going to go home.'

Where was he going to get money from? Money and food. The hunger burned inside him so much he could hardly stand upright. His digestive juices were eating him from the inside. He had started to eat himself up. Mik went into ICA and hid two chocolate wafer bars and a bottle of Coke under his T-shirt. They weren't invisible, exactly, and the man on the till grabbed him at the exit. A hard grip on his neck.

'What have you got there?'

'I'm hungry.'

'Come with me.'

He was made to sit at a table in a small room with the stolen goods in front of him. They asked him his name and address. Mik said nothing. He stared at the chocolate wafers and the Coke.

'Telephone number,' said the man from the till. 'Come on, there's a good lad, so we can get this sorted. We're closing soon and I want to go home. Give me the number and I'll phone and ask your parents to come and get you. That's how we usually deal with this kind of thing.'

'I haven't got a number.'

'Haven't you got a telephone at home? No mobile?'

'They've changed the lock and name plate. H. Stål.'

'Now come on, what's your phone number? Stop messing about. You must have parents. A mum and a dad.'

'No.'

~~~

The staff at ICA got nowhere with the shoplifter. They threatened and bargained until finally they managed to get a number out of him, but that line rental was no longer in existence. They kept him there until the shop closed. A bit of confusion arose about what to do with him. Should someone take him home with them, perhaps? They could hardly just let him go; that would be tricky too. Would give completely the wrong signals. But they thought it seemed unkind to ring the police just for two chocolate wafer bars. That's what Mik thought too.

But unfortunately he didn't have a phone number to give them. Mik shrugged his shoulders and asked if he could have one of the chocolate wafers because he was really hungry and hadn't eaten all day. They said he could, and then the police turned up. Two big men, dressed in black, with noisy footsteps.

Mik became frightened. They had pistols and heavy boots and looked like two of Tengil's evil soldiers. They were going to brand his backside with the mark of Katla the dragon.

'Well, well,' one of them said. 'Is this the chocolate wafer thief?'

Mik stuffed the last piece into his mouth. Swallowed and said quietly, 'I was given this one, and if I'm given the other one then I won't have taken anything.'

'Yes, you have. The Coke,' said the cashier wearily. 'We want to go home now. The shop's closed. We've finished for the day.'

'Well, phone the parents, for heaven's sake. They can come and get him,' said the other policeman.

'That's just the problem. He's been sitting here for four hours and he hasn't told us his name, address or number.'

Mik was given the other chocolate wafer too. And the Coke. He drank that while he was in the police car.

FROM THE GRAVE

They hadn't branded the mark of Katla onto his backside. They found out who he was pretty quickly. That he was on the run from a foster home in Bro, and the family were missing him very much.

He slept in a police cell with the door open. That was the first time he hadn't had to sleep locked in for a long time. Early the following morning, Parrot Earrings drove him back. He sat in the back seat and she droned on and on throughout the whole journey.

She said Mik had behaved stupidly and many people had been worried. They thought he had drowned. Mik tried to tell her what an awful place it was. That they were tormentors.

'I can't believe that,' she said, looking at him in the rear-view mirror.

Her shoulder bag lay on the back seat next to Mik.

'The food's disgusting,' said Mik, noticing the bag was open. 'I have to clean up dog shit.'

'Well, of course you have to help out there. It's fun looking after animals.'

'I don't like animals.'

'This is the best family. You'll get used to it. Everything will be fine.'

'No,' said Mik, sliding his hand over the seat and into her bag.

'You've got to understand, this is the best thing for you.'

His hand searched and felt. A bunch of keys, a mobile, a box of tablets, throat sweets, maybe. Glasses case. Purse.

~~~

Mik arrived back in time for breakfast. Parrot Earrings was in a hurry and left immediately.

He was given cornflakes and milk. Rickard pulled out a chair. He sat opposite Mik, leaning his elbows on the table and resting his chin on his knuckles. He was wearing a sleeveless top and his biceps bulged. Mik looked down into his bowl of cereal.

'Jasack died last night. His heart. He didn't get his heart medication, did he?'

'I forgot,' said Mik.

'And now he's dead.'

Rickard was silent for a while and looked seriously at Mik. A hard, blue gaze. The spoon shook; milk slopped out.

'He's going to lie on the hill beyond the stables. The highest one, with the tall juniper bush. You'll find the spade in the tool-shed, and I want you to dig a proper grave. At least a metre deep.'

~~~

Steel hit stone. The spade shuddered in his hands and there was a smell of burning. The sun beat down from a cloud-free sky. It was as hot as the desert. The punishment, thought Mik. The prisoner is digging his own grave and will be made

203

to stand on the edge and be shot. A neat descent into the grave. But someone else would have to put the earth back in the hole. A blindfold for the eyes and a last cigarette.

For three days he had been working on it. It was unbelievably stony. Jasack would have time to rot before it was finished. Stones and more stones. His body ached. Blisters came up on his hands and burst. Mik took a break, drank water from a plastic bottle and stared up at the sun. The light shimmered through the water. He stood in the grave and the vultures circled overhead, waiting for death. Glided with wings outstretched.

Mik took off his T-shirt, tied it round his head and carried on digging. The sweat ran. The spade came up against a large rock. He kneeled down and worked it free with his hands until his nails split. It was to be a neat grave, with nice, straight sides. And deep, so the dog wouldn't be able to climb back into this world again.

A shadow fell across him.

'Hello, down there in the grave.'

It was Niklas standing up there, outlined in the sunlight, his rifle in his hand.

'Have a look at this weird old bird I've shot. Fat and ugly.'

Niklas held it up by the legs so that the wings hung straight out, making it look like an upside-down cross.

'It was sitting in the top of a tree. It died immediately. A perfect shot.'

He threw it down in the grave at Mik's feet. It had a large head and yellow eyes. Its body was brown with black and

white stripes across the chest. It was a hawk owl. Mik threw
down the spade, climbed up out of the grave and ran towards
the forest.

~~~

The rails shone in the sunshine and the air quivered over the
tracks. He was out of breath and his heart pounded.

There was 425 kronor in Parrot Earrings' purse. He took
out the money and threw the purse far away into the forest.

~~~

The bus stopped at the little square. The brakes hissed and
the doors opened. Mik was the only passenger to get off. He
had no luggage.

'Nothing?' said the driver, who had already climbed out
and opened the door of the luggage hatch.

'No, nothing,' said Mik and looked around. 'But is this
really Selet?'

The birch trees were green; there was grass and flower
borders. It was all so unfamiliar.

'You've come to the right place. Isn't anyone coming to
meet you?'

'I'll be okay.'

The driver climbed back into the bus, closed the doors
and drove away.

The Konsum sign had gone but the word Konsum could
still be made out in ghostly writing on the outside wall. A
car drove past; a lawnmower started up.

Mik looked around, anxious that someone might be

following him. That they were on his trail. Bloodhounds. Tengil's men. But there was no one to be seen.

He passed the school and came onto the bridge. The river glittered in the sun. The water ran freely and fish splashed on the surface. Far below in the river-bend someone was fishing and caught something. A wriggling fish flew through the air.

'WOOF!'

Gustavsson's dog stood in front of him. Growled, the hair on its back standing on end. Mik stared it straight in the eyes and said, 'Quiet.'

The dog was absolutely stunned.

'Sit.'

It sat.

Lena's house stood wrapped in leafy green trees and the gravel path up to the front steps was lined with flower-beds. The grass was long and growing wild. He walked straight in. Lena was sitting at the kitchen table, sorting tablets for the Selström brothers' tablet boxes. She looked up.

'Mik?'

'Yes.'

'But …?'

And then she smiled and held out her arms.

He started to cry. His whole body shook. He rushed up to her and she hugged him tightly. Everything went warm and his body relaxed and softened, as if his skeleton had dissolved.

'Goodness, how dirty you are.'

'I've come from the grave.'

PART 5

THE RAFT

A HERO

Lena laid the table for breakfast. Mik ate cheese roll after cheese roll, dipped in his hot chocolate until the cheese melted into strings. Suddenly Pi was standing in the kitchen. She smiled.

She had changed. Something was missing. The blue birthmark on her cheek had gone. Instead only a red patch could be seen on her suntanned face.

'The mark's gone,' said Mik.

'Looks good, doesn't it?'

'I don't know. It looks empty.'

Pi laughed, sat down and helped herself to a cheese roll.

'How did you know I was here?' said Mik.

'Everyone knows you're here. I saw you yesterday on the bridge. I waved, but you didn't wave back.'

'Was that you, fishing?'

'Yep. Do you want to go to the lake for a swim?'

Mik nodded with his mouth full and hot chocolate running down his chin. But then he remembered.

'Swimming shorts?'

Lena made a pair. She cut the legs off the dirty, ripped jeans. Took the scissors and chopped them off just above the knee. She would organise new clothes for him during the day.

Lake Selet didn't have a real beach, not a nice one with sand gently sloping into the lake. The forest hugged the lakeside, leaning over water that was black and that got suddenly very deep. The shoreline sloped steeply, covered in roots and rocks from landslides.

Pi changed under her towel using a complicated arm and leg routine to wriggle into her swimming costume so that Mik would not get even the tiniest glimpse of her naked body.

'You've just got to dive from the edge,' said Pi.

'Oh,' said Mik and took off his shoes and top. He looked at her and she looked at him. She smiled and struggled, bent over on one leg under her towel.

'Are you going to stay here now?'

'Yes.'

'That's good,' said Pi and dropped the towel to the ground.

'Lots of ants here,' said Mik. 'And mosquitoes.'

'Jump in, then.'

'No, I'll wait a bit.'

A long, thick tree trunk floated past, a short way from land.

'Oh, we've got to have that,' said Pi.

'What?'

'That log. Come on.'

She dived in neatly and effortlessly. No big splash, just a little gurgle. She was sucked under the surface and glided a long way below the water before surfacing. She shook her head and water flew from her hair in the sunshine. With a few rapid strokes she reached the log and hung her arms over it.

'Come on, Mik. I can't bring it in on my own. Jump in.'

Ants crawled over his feet and he lifted them up and down on the spot.

'Wimp. It's not cold. You get used to it.'

Pi clambered onto the log and performed a little balancing act, standing on it and waving her arms around. She fell in with a splash. She snorted and laughed.

'Help me. It's not cold. The log's important.'

Mik scattered a few ants into the water. They floated.

'We've got to get it up on land.'

Pi climbed up again and balanced. The log rolled, her legs crossed and she fell in. Splash.

'How deep is it?'

'A few metres. Five, maybe. I've never been down to the bottom. Oskar has.'

'Okay.'

Mik jumped in. He thrashed about, tried a crawl stroke, started to twist and turn and sank. It got rapidly darker and colder. His eyes ached, the pressure increased and then he heard the note getting louder, heard the whale song. It was inside his head. It was his own note in his ear, made louder by the pressure. Did he have a whale in his head? Was that possible?

Pi came swimming down to him, getting lighter and lighter. Her face was up against his, her hair billowing. It floated about down there in a golden curtain of sun-rays. His lungs started to go into a cramp but he didn't panic. It was beautiful.

Pi shook her head, pulled a silly face and wrapped her arms around him. They floated up to the surface.

Mik had swallowed water and his forehead pounded. Pi laid her towel across his shoulders.

'You can't swim. Why didn't you say so? Why did you jump in?'

'I didn't want to look retarded and stupid.'

'So you jumped in instead. And that's not the slightest bit retarded and stupid? Five metres deep. What did you expect, a miracle?'

Filip and Oskar came running between the trees down to the beach. Oskar bombarded Mik with questions. Had he moved here? Was he going to live here now? Where had he been?

Mik told them the truth. He was on the run from the Tormentors.

Oskar was impressed and asked, 'Did you dig an escape tunnel?'

'No, I was only locked in at night.'

Filip looked dubious and stood unnecessarily close to Pi.

'It's not that hard to escape,' he said sullenly. 'Anyone can do it.'

'The log!' shouted Pi. 'It's drifting away. We've got to get it in.'

Pi, Oskar and Filip dived in and rapidly swam out to begin the laborious task of barging the log to the shore. Pi was in charge, and the log moved slowly towards land. Mik felt absolutely useless and sat on the edge of the lake, flicking ants into the water.

Oskar and Filip wondered why he didn't help with the log instead of sitting there among the ants.

'He can't swim,' said Pi.

Pi, Oskar and Filip had collected about ten large logs throughout the summer. They lay tied together on the lake shore to stop them drifting away. Some floated high in the water; others floated lower.

Pi had collected lengths of rope in different colours and thicknesses which were used to tie the logs together. They had to be bound tightly. It was going to be a raft.

'It's going to be a big one,' said Oskar. He was trying to tie a knot but it kept coming undone.

Pi was in charge of the work. She and Mik worked on top of the raft, lashing the logs together. Oskar and Filip had the job of diving down and passing the rope under the logs, and their heads popped up and down like fishing floats with a fish on the end. Mik grabbed the ropes handed to him by the divers and Pi tied all the knots.

As soon as Oskar came up out of the water, his mouth started working. Mik could see him talking even under the water, although only bubbles came out. He wanted to know everything about running away and what it was like. Whether it was cool or scary and if there was anything you had to think about when you ran away. Was there a manual? Handy tips and advice?

'First you have to know where you're going,' said Mik.

'But you're running away from something, aren't you?' said Oskar.

'Maybe,' said Mik. 'But if you don't know where you're going it gets confusing very quickly.'

'What's the most important thing?'

'Food, water and money. Otherwise you'd easily give up.'

'Did you have that?' asked Filip, who had started to weaken.

'No, not the first time.'

'You've run away more than once?'

'Yes, but then the police caught me.'

'Is that true?' said Filip. 'The police?'

Mik felt himself swell with pride. Even moody Filip was impressed. It was an unfamiliar feeling. Just like having a little glowing jewel in your chest.

He told them about everything that had happened to him. Killer dogs and dog turds. How he had been taken by the police but had been allowed to keep the chocolate wafer biscuits and the Coke. And how he had buried a massive great dog.

Mik was a hero, no doubt about it. That's what they thought, all three of them.

Pi often brushed against him while they were binding one log to the next. Their hands met when they tightened and fastened the ropes.

Filip and Oskar continually popped up out of the water with more questions. Some things they wanted to hear a second time. Over and over again he had to tell them how he cleaned up the dog mess and threw up in his porridge. And what about that thing with the chocolate wafers and the Coke? Amazing that he had been allowed to keep something he had stolen.

Not one of them doubted what he said was true. Filip was a bit sceptical about some of the details. Pi didn't ask very much. She listened, mainly, and prodded him along a little.

'Did you go in a police car?'

'Yes.'

'With a flashing blue light and a siren?'

'No.'

'Handcuffs, then?'

'No, the police were nice.'

Mik told them about spying on a naked girl.

Oskar and Filip stopped working and dangled in the water, their arms crossed on top of the raft.

He showed them the whip marks, which were still visible as blue lines.

'Shi-i-it,' said Oskar. 'Did you see everything? Did you see her bush?'

'Yes.'

Pi didn't like that.

'Just drop it, would you? Get back to your diving. That's enough. We've heard it all. Pull the rope, and then we need another one at the back. Dive now.'

But they didn't dive. They hung onto the raft and wanted to hear more.

'Her breasts,' said Oskar. 'Were they like –?'

Pi flicked a piece of blue rope in the air. Oskar cried out in pain. It had hit him across the neck. She was pleased with her aim.

'You've already heard what happened.'

'Okay, okay, calm down,' said Filip. 'But how deep did you dig the dog grave?'

'Two metres. At least,' said Mik.

'You're a hero,' said Oskar and rubbed his neck where a vivid red mark was appearing.

'But I can't swim,' said Mik.

'No, but you're going to learn,' said Pi.

The swimming lessons started on dry land. Mik had to lie down on his stomach and make swimming strokes in thin air. Pine needles, twigs and cones dug into his skin. Pi showed him what to do and corrected his mistakes.

'You mustn't forget the leg movements just because you're moving your arms, and vice versa,' she said.

It was difficult. When he concentrated on the leg movements, he forgot his arms. And huge ants crawled all over him.

Filip and Oskar helped with the lesson. Mik laughed as he lay on the ground, flinging his arms about. Oskar leapt around, clowning. Filip showed off, saying he could do all the swimming strokes. Pi stood there, pointing and in charge. It was fun and released something in his body. He became calm and still. He had come home.

The swimming on dry land became better and better. Good, wide swimming strokes. Soon only the fine-tuning remained.

'You're a swimming expert,' said Oskar.

'Hmm. On land,' said Filip.

Pi told him to jump in and swim along the edge of the water. Mik jumped in, flailed about and sank.

Pi dragged him out and said, 'We need rope. Get some from the raft.'

Filip fetched some rope, which they tied around Mik's waist, and they guided him along the edge, pulling him up when he sank, which he did as soon as they let the line go slack.

'Slow, steady strokes,' said Pi. 'Wide, slow strokes.'

But Mik didn't hear. He had sunk. They lifted him up and held the rope taut.

'Come on,' yelled Filip. 'Don't sink.'

'Look. A metre, at least,' said Oskar.

Mik sank. He was utterly exhausted. They pulled him up. He coughed and spluttered and was freezing cold.

'Right,' said Pi. 'This could take some time.'

~~~

It was evening. Mik sat in his attic room and looked out through the window, scratching his mosquito bites. Everything looked different now, in the summertime. Soft and green. The sun hadn't gone down, even though it was late. It was almost as light as the middle of the day, but more yellowish. Bengt and Bertil came out with their potties.

The hawk owl was not sitting in the tree.

A creaking came from the stairs. Lena was carrying a tray with milk and sandwiches. He ate as she watched.

'No owl,' said Mik with his mouth full. He pointed towards the window with his sandwich.

'It rarely sits there in the summer.'

'Do they fly far?'

'No, I don't think so. Have the brothers peed?'

'Yes,' said Mik.

'You see, everything here is just the same.'

'Konsum,' said Mik, taking another sandwich.

'Well, yes. I do my shopping at ICA now.'

'Cheese,' said Mik. 'Cheese is nice. The Tormentors didn't give me any cheese.'

There were no sandwiches left. Mik wriggled down under the duvet and pulled it up until it just covered his nose. Lena stood up and took the tray. She looked at him, shook her head and laughed.

'In time they'll realise you are here. But until then …'

'I don't want to go back.'

GETTING THE RAFT READY

Lena had found clothes for him. Second-hand, faded and completely impossible. But here no one cared what they looked like. The summer days were hot, the sky blue and the night light. The water in Lake Selet was horribly cold and there were masses of mosquitoes, gnats and ants. Lena rubbed a cooling ointment into his skin every evening.

Pi was extremely stubborn about the swimming lessons. Mik swallowed water, vomited and suffered from the cold. But she didn't give up. It was as if she was on a mission from God to teach him to swim. But he sank.

'Perhaps he's too thin,' said Oskar. 'Unable to float. He kind of falls through.'

Filip had brought along his little sister's swimming ring, a ridiculous thing that went around his waist and had two yellow floats on the back so that only your legs and head sank. Oskar thought it was a step forward, and when Pi was out of earshot he wanted to hear about spying on the naked girl.

'Did you really see her bush?'

'Yes, I saw everything.'

～～

The raft turned out well. All four of them could stand on it without it sinking even a little bit.

Filip ordered planks from his dad. They made a flat floor so that Pi's tent could be put up on the raft. They nailed the tent ropes and the eyelets that held the canvas in place. It was perfect.

Bengt and Bertil gave them worn-out old oars as paddles. Finally they hoisted a mast with a flag that Oskar had made.

'Skull and crossbones,' he said.

But it looked more like a grinning clown.

One night they slept in the tent on the raft after paddling over to the other side of the lake. It took several hours, and night fell before they got there. The raft floated heavily through the water. Filip became tired and whiny, but that might have been because he had a cold and a runny nose.

'Where else are we going to go on this thing?' he said, sniffing. 'Backwards and forwards over the lake or what? How cool is that?'

'We can travel out into the world,' said Oskar. 'Run away.'

'How? This raft weighs a ton. It can't fly.'

The sun set, but it didn't get dark; it was only like coming into the shade. The air was coloured blue, and far in the distance were the mountain tops, still in sunlight. Mik thought the mountains looked as if they were made of solid gold.

'The river,' said Pi. 'It runs into the sea. And from the sea you can travel out into the world.'

'To China,' said Oskar.

'Well, yes, actually.'

'Cool,' said Filip. 'The raft will be crushed going over the Älg rapids.'

They crawled into the tent and rolled around among airbeds, blankets, covers and pillows. Mik borrowed one of Pi's pillows.

Filip's mobile rang. It was his mum, wondering if everything was going well. She said, 'Big kiss and sleep tight,' and everyone heard. Oskar and Pi switched off their phones, not wanting to run the risk of getting phone calls like that.

'This raft won't have any problem with the Älg rapids,' said Pi. 'I'm sure about that. As long as no one falls off.'

'What about the Borg rapids, then?' said Filip.

'No problem,' said Pi. 'But everyone must be able to swim. For Mik it could be dangerous.'

'Then what?' said Oskar.

'I don't know what's going to happen after that,' said Pi.

Mik listened to their conversation, not word for word but more as a noise going on in the background. Lovely voices. He liked Pi's best; it was a bit hoarse. Filip's was squeaky. Oskar's voice was slurred somehow, as if his tongue was a bit too big for his mouth.

They argued about what the raft could and couldn't handle. It felt secure to lie there and listen. He wasn't alone and he would never have to be alone again. Mik fell asleep on Pi's pillow to the sound of the voices.

The next morning it was Mik's swimming practice. He

swam beside the raft with a rope and the ridiculous float around his waist.

'That's good,' said Pi. 'Long, slow strokes. And keep your fingers together so you get a grip in the water.'

The lessons went so well they decided to practise without the float. Mik jumped in, sank and bobbed about with puffed cheeks.

'Fish him out,' said Pi pointing down into the water.

Oskar and Filip dived in and dragged him up onto the raft.

'For goodness' sake,' said Pi and made a wavy, irritated gesture with her arms.

'Uuuugghhh,' spluttered Mik.

He tried again. For some reason he panicked and went too fast and sank again.

'Self-confidence,' said Pi. 'Where's your self-confidence? You little Peeping Tom, you. Well?'

They paddled the raft back over the lake. A light headwind meant that it took them the rest of the day. Filip thought they ought to get hold of an outboard motor.

Synchro-Bertil came rowing up with an odd-looking hat on his head.

'Fine vessel you have there,' he said.

'It's a raft,' said Oskar.

Synchro-Bertil rested on his oars.

'Things don't have to be the way they appear. Your raft

might not be a raft. It might be the Silver Ark, come to carry people up into heaven. And you are angels.'

Synchro-Bertil heaved up his oars, bent down and lifted up a pike.

'Here is a pike. But I ask you, is it really a pike? How can you be certain? Reality is built on deeper, more profound coincidences, unknown to us. You see a raft, I see the Silver Ark.'

'Yes,' said Filip. 'And your boat is perhaps a banana.'

'Exactly,' said Synchro-Bertil and rowed on.

The raft worked. Now it had to be made ready, said Pi.

'For what?' said Filip.

'The Great Escape,' said Pi.

'Yes,' said Oskar. 'Let's run away.'

Mik said nothing.

They were all going to help to get everything that was needed. Pi made a list. Saucepans, tins of food, fishing rod, compass. It turned out to be a long list. They lugged things and stowed them in boxes on the raft, and Pi crossed them off the list.

'Tin opener and box of plasters,' said Mik.

'Good,' said Pi. 'Here's a fishing rod, line and hooks.'

Filip had binoculars and Oskar a bow and arrows. He was going to hunt if they ran short of food.

'With a bow and arrow?' said Filip.

'Yes.'

'Are you going to shoot frogs then or what?'

'Elk, maybe,' said Oskar.

'The arrow would bounce back and hit you in the forehead.'

'No, not if I hit the elk in the eye.'

'You wouldn't be able to shoot an elk if it was three metres away.'

'Stop it,' said Pi. 'The most important thing is the food we take with us.'

She went through all the tins they had brought from home: meatballs, peas, beans, tomato soup, sweetcorn, stew and pineapple. They even had a whole packet of macaroni and some boxes of raisins. The raft was full of supplies and ready to go. They would run away as soon as Mik learned to swim.

THE PARAGRAPH

Bengt and Mik sat at the kitchen table doing a crossword. The words were difficult and they were stuck on one clue: herb among rose plants, eight letters. Bengt looked at Mik over the top of his glasses.

'Doris Day.'

'Doris who?' said Mik.

'We were going to watch a film with Doris Day.'

Bengt stood up, went into the sitting room and started rooting through his videos. Finally he found the right tape and inserted it into the video player. Mik was given a cushion and lay down on the floor. The film began on the big Trinitron screen.

April in Paris.

Mik didn't understand a thing. Well, he understood the story, but not what was so good about it. It was a blurry old film in weird colours and everyone behaved stupidly. As for Doris herself, she burst into song in the most ridiculous places in the story. It was unrealistic, and where was the music coming from? Pianos and violins and trumpets. Who was playing? And there were no special effects whatsoever.

'What a woman,' said Bengt.

She was really old, but Mik didn't say that.

The film came to an end, Bengt switched off the video player and the News leapt onto the TV screen. That was when Mik saw the most incredible thing he had ever seen. If Doris Day was unrealistic, bursting into song with an invisible piano and trumpets, she was nothing compared with this. The big thirty-two inch Trinitron showed a picture of Mik himself. The picture was a school photo and a voice was droning from the loudspeaker. He heard what it said. He heard his name mentioned and that he had disappeared. But he didn't understand.

Bengt had frozen, bent over with his finger still on the video on/off button. Then it was gone and the news continued, with starving children, desert war, floods and burning embassies.

Bengt stretched upright, resting his hands on his lower back.

'Well I'll be damned,' he said. 'You're a celebrity. I've got a celebrity in the house. On the TV and everything. Now you can bet your life the telephone lines in the village will be red-hot, what with all the old women in the village ringing round. This'll be enough to keep them going for several years.'

Mik didn't understand what it was that would keep them going; he didn't understand anything. He gulped and gulped. Something was trying to come up out of his stomach. Not food. Not sick. It was something else. His very heart, perhaps.

'It'll be all right,' said Bengt. 'Everything will sort itself out. You know, everything blows over and every one of us is dying. So why worry? You coming with me tomorrow to bring up the nets?'

Mik gulped and gulped. He left without saying goodbye.

The very same evening Mik had been on television, the police phoned from Umeå and asked Lena if he was with her. Cautiously she asked what made them think that. Well, there had been no less than twelve phone calls from people in Selet to the Umeå police concerning Mik.

Lena couldn't lie. That would have just made everything worse. She put down the receiver slowly and calmly and looked at Mik.

'Twelve?' she said. 'Well, at least we know how many old blabbermouths we've got in the village.'

Mik was in total shock. He lay in his bed thinking the police would arrive any minute. Lena sat with him.

'No,' she said. 'They won't come now, and probably not tomorrow, either. It can take a while. They wanted to know if you were well and if everything was okay.'

'But they will come?' said Mik from under the duvet.

'Yes, they will come.'

She sat with him until he fell asleep.

The next morning Parrot Earrings rang. She didn't ask anything about Mik, nothing about how he was or what he thought. She was offended and angry that Lena hadn't got in touch immediately when Mik turned up. That she had hidden him for so long.

'Hidden?' said Lena. 'He came here and wanted to live here, and I let him.'

It was a long conversation. Lena was very cool and calm as she spoke with Parrot Earrings. Of course Lena could apply to be Mik's guardian, but Parrot Earrings couldn't promise anything because a new, detailed enquiry had to be carried out.

Mik listened to the entire conversation. Lena held the phone so he could hear what Parrot Earrings said. A lot of it was hard to understand.

Lena would be sent all the application forms and papers needed for an enquiry, but while that was happening Mik had to go back to the foster home. As soon as possible.

'Why?' said Lena.

'It's been decided. It's a CiC: a Children in Care order. And you have to follow the law. What would it look like otherwise? We are responsible for him.'

'But he's happy here.'

'The decision was made by social services. Are you questioning the competence of the authorities?'

'Not at all,' said Lena. She ended the conversation politely and calmly and then put down the phone.

'CiC?' said Mik.

'Cunning. Incompetent. Clowns,' said Lena.

Oskar, Filip and Pi were incredibly impressed. Mik had been on TV as a missing person. This was big, bigger than when the ice melted and swept away the bridge four years ago. It was bigger than when Bengt shot the Nygård wolf and was given six months in prison for illegal hunting. Or when Synchro-Bertil built an enormous landing strip for a UFO on the top of Granberg mountain.

Twelve people who couldn't wait to pick up their phones and ring Tengil's men in Umeå. Of course, Bengt had said, that was obvious. TV had a huge impact and he was dead certain he could make a list of the people who had phoned. But Bengt said that Mik should let it go.

'The blasted old gossips are bored to death in a quiet village like this. You've given their lives meaning up until next Christmas at least. We men have got fishing and hunting, but those old women can only peer through the geraniums on their window sills, desperately wishing something would happen. And the only thing that happens is that spring turns to summer and summer to autumn and autumn to winter. And so it goes on.'

Mik slept badly and woke covered in sweat. At first he thought he had wet himself, or wet himself all over. Totally.

Lena explained it was the kind of thing that happened when you were worried and afraid. Warm milk with honey helped. She boiled up very hot milk with honey in it.

Mik went with Bengt out onto Lake Selet to bring up the

nets. The oars creaked. Mik said nothing. They rowed past the raft which was tied up on the beach.

'Fine construction,' said Bengt. 'Biggest raft that has ever sailed on Lake Selet.'

Mik didn't answer. He dangled one hand in the water and was watching the trail it made.

They reached the marker buoy and Bengt began to heave up the net. Mik took care with the rowing. It didn't go too well. He made the boat turn left when it should have turned right. They went backwards when they should have gone forwards. The oars got in a muddle and wouldn't do what they were supposed to do, but Bengt was as patient as Baloo. They caught a few pike, but they weren't as large as the winter ones.

'Ice dragons,' said Mik. 'This winter we'll fish for ice dragons, won't we?'

'Yes,' said Bengt.

'Promise me I'll still be here, catching ice dragons with you.'

'Of course, I promise. You can hide in my house if they come. We'll load the gun and then just let them try. I've shot both bear and wolf.'

He laughed.

It was a bad catch that day but it felt good to be with Bengt, to sit there in the boat, swaying to the movement of the oars. And out here on the water no one could take him by surprise. His vision was clear in all directions. On the other side of the lake, Synchro-Bertil was rowing.

'Why don't you talk to each other?' asked Mik.

'He's an idiot and speaks in riddles.'

'Yes, but what he says is exciting.'

'Exciting?' said Bengt, and rested on the oars.

'Yes, that the cosmos is only an idea and that a pike doesn't necessarily have to be a pike.'

'He's lost his mind. That's the talk of a genuine fool.'

'My brother's gone,' said Mik. 'I've written masses of letters but he never answers.'

'Could be something wrong with the post,' said Bengt.

Mik lay along the prow of the boat, his face looking down into the water. He saw his own reflection and thought of Tony. Was he dead or what?

'As for the post,' said Bengt. 'It isn't what it was once. Perhaps your brother hasn't even received the letters. There have actually been letters that have taken twenty years to arrive.'

Mik caught a white water lily and the stalk came off with a pling, like an elastic band. It was for Lena. Or Pi. No, that would be stupid. Lena could have it.

'The water lily only opens when the sun shines,' said Bengt. 'On cloudy days it stays shut. That's good. Make the most of the sunny days; don't bother about the rest.'

'That sounded just like Synchro-Bertil.'

'Did it? That can't be possible.'

'I wish Tony was here. There's so much I'd like to tell him and show him.'

Bengt stopped rowing. Water dropped from the oars. He looked out over the lake.

'I wish my brother would fall out of his boat over there on the other side and get tangled up in his nets and sink to the bottom.'

Mik dropped the water lily into the water but quickly scooped it out again.

'What, so that he drowns and dies?'

'No, so I can save the old devil and make it quits.'

～～～

Lena was sent the application forms. She worked on them all evening at the kitchen table. Read and wrote. Mik was allowed to read what she had written but didn't understand much. The water lily stood in a vase on the table. The flower was closed.

'Good Lord,' said Lena and looked around the untidy kitchen. 'They want to know everything.'

'Write that it's the best living here. Best place in the world. Write that Synchro-Bertil has built a landing place for the UFO.'

'It's me they want to know about. My home will be inspected. Personal interviews. They're going to turn everything inside out and check my entire life.'

'Do they have to know everything? Is there someone who knows everything?'

'Yes, unfortunately. If you lie, they'll find out, and then we're done for. I won't be approved.'

'But you're good,' said Mik. 'I approve of you.'

'Oh, if only it were that simple,' said Lena and rattled off, 'Partner, living alone, alcohol, drugs, finances and … oh shit.'

'What?' said Mik.

'Nothing, it's just that there's so much of it. Listen to this: "An enquiry that will form the basis for a decision about custody must be objective, impartial and truthful, according to the Constitution, Chapter one, Paragraph nine."'

'Paragraph?'

'It's bedtime,' said Lena.

Mik creaked slowly up the stairs. He stood extra long on the stair that creaked the most.

'Paragraph,' he said slowly and in the same tone as the creak.

And then the next stair.

'Paragraph.'

And the next.

'Paragraph.'

And the next.

'Parrot Earrings.'

'Parrot Earrings.'

'Parrot Earrings.'

He would like to lure her up to Granberg mountains where Bertil had built his landing strip and let the UFO take her.

THEY'RE HERE NOW

Mik was having a swimming lesson, attached to a rope from the bridge. He fought against the current, fought against the river of primeval rivers which flowed from the mountain of primeval mountains. Water gushed towards him, was forced into his ears and mouth. Pushed its way up his nose, filled his forehead and the whole of his brain. His arm and leg muscles screamed.

It had been Oskar's idea. At first everyone had thought it was crazy.

'Yes, but,' he said, 'if Mik swims against the current we only have to stand on the bridge and hold the rope. He won't go anywhere.'

Filip laughed. Pi thought for a while and said, 'You're a genius, Oskar.'

'Am I?' said Oskar.

So Mik lay there, struggling, putting in as much effort as he could manage. Squeezed the last bit of strength out of every muscle. It wasn't enough. The current was pushing him backwards. The rope chafed his stomach. Oskar was an idiot.

Pi held the rope up on the bridge. She shouted, 'Fight! Keep your fingers together. Long strokes or you'll be dragged along with it.'

'Legs,' yelled Filip. 'Don't forget your legs.'

Mik bent over double and was swept under the bridge. Pi had to run down to the bridge footings and pull him ashore. Mik crawled up onto the bank, snorted and hissed and felt like a spineless water animal. His muscles quivered.

'It was a good idea, but you probably have to know how to swim to be able to do it.'

Oskar helped Mik up onto his feet.

'So I'm not a genius?'

Mik put his clothes on and they clambered up the slope. A silver-coloured car drove across the bridge. It was going fast and flashed by. Dust from the road whirled in the air. A shining silver flash of lightning out of a clear blue summer sky. Right into the heart.

Mik had known it would happen, but for safety's sake his brain had hidden it away in the security room, the same place where death lived.

Now the steel doors flew open and everything poured out, all jumbled up. Dog turds, skeletons, monsters, dysfunctional foster parents, spiders, H. Stål and Snake Alone. They crawled around inside him in a brown sludge.

Gold Tooth was driving and Parrot Earrings sat beside him. They hadn't seen him. The car drove over the bridge and continued past Gustavsson's dog, which launched a violent attack. It chased after them, barking, until it came to the end of its leash. The dog whirled round with a strangled cry and landed on its back.

If the cosmos was only a thought, there was no more thinking to be done. The world had ended.

'Mik, what is it?' said Pi. 'Have you hurt yourself? Was it the rope?'

His tendons wouldn't hold him up. His knees gave way and he fell into Pi's arms.

'They're here now.'

Immediately she understood, held him hard and looked away towards the car that turned off the road to Lena's house.

'Breathe,' she said, close to his ear.

'I am breathing.'

'Good,' said Pi quietly. 'We'll sort this out. You know that. We'll run off.'

Oskar had no idea what was going on. He thought it was his fault. That something had happened to Mik during his swimming lesson. That something had been broken.

'Is he injured?'

'Don't you get it?' said Filip. 'Mik's got to go back to the darkness. To the concentration camp to clean up the dog shit. To the evil side.'

They all looked towards the road junction where the car had disappeared. Gustavsson's dog got back on its feet, vomited a little and loped back to his kennel.

'Are we the good side?' said Oskar.

'You're the bonkers side,' said Filip.

'The raft,' said Pi.

THE PARAGRAPH FLIES

The raft felt heavier and slower than ever before. They glided forward as if through treacle, even though there was a following wind out on the lake. Mik, Oskar and Filip were on their knees, paddling in silence. The tent canvas rustled gently; the waves lapped against the logs.

Pi stood up, binoculars to her eyes, sweeping the edges of the lake. They had paddled first straight across Lake Selet and then followed the shoreline towards the end of the lake where it flowed into the river. Filip had protested, saying the route would be quicker if they paddled directly towards the end of the lake.

'Of course we could do that,' Pi had said, 'if you want them to see us straight away. If we follow the other edge we won't be seen against the forest.'

Pi swept the lakeside again. She couldn't see any possible threat, so she lowered the binoculars and said, 'Okay. We're running away.'

'But Mik's already running away,' said Oskar. 'Now he's running away from running away.'

'Shut up,' said Pi.

'The double runner,' said Oskar and laughed at his own joke.

'Double genius,' said Filip.

The hours went by and it felt as if they were getting nowhere. Silence covered the forest of ancient gnarled trees lining the shore. The branches hung over the water as if they were trying to snare the raft, and deeper into the dense darkness a tangle of dead trees with their uprooted trunks could be made out, like giant watchful spiders.

'I'm too tired to do any more,' whined Filip.

'Paddle,' said Pi.

Filip looked at his hands.

'I've got blisters and my shoulder's twisted out of its socket.'

'It'll be better later,' said Pi. 'Once we reach the river we'll only have to go with the current and steer.'

But Filip carried on moaning. 'Where are we heading, then?'

'To China,' said Oskar, grinning.

'We're running away from something,' said Pi. 'Not to something. Whatever happens, happens.'

'What will happen then?' said Oskar.

'We'll die in the Älg rapids,' said Filip.

'I don't want to die,' said Oskar.

Pi got annoyed. 'You're such flipping cowards.'

'I'm a coward, am I?' yelled Filip, and he let go of the paddle and clenched his fists.

'Yes,' said Pi. 'You didn't even dare take Maria's cat back.'

'Stop it,' said Mik. 'You can let me off at the shore and I'll go on my own.'

'Where?' said Oskar.

'Somewhere.'

It was a game for them, but it was no game for him. The difference was enormous and endless, and nothing could be done about it. It was he and he alone who was being hunted by The Paragraph. When Pi, Filip and Oskar got tired of the game they could creep down into their own beds and call for warm milk. He understood them. No one was a coward. You needed courage to be able to face a threat, and to risk danger when there was no threat wasn't brave but stupid.

'Just help me to paddle the raft ashore and I'll go on my own.'

Pi, Filip and Oskar stood looking at Mik in silence as he paddled the raft with all his strength without moving it any closer to the shore. The muscles in his thin arms were tensed, his neck was bent. He put his whole body into the effort. Heaved and sobbed. The raft didn't move.

Pi's mobile started to ring. One ring, two. She picked it up and looked at the display. Three rings, four. Everyone looked at her. Five rings. She held her hand out over the edge of the raft and let go of the phone. Splash. They stared at her in astonishment, their eyes wide. She smiled back. Oskar's phone started to ring. He looked at Pi, grinned uncertainly and threw it in.

Seconds later there was a ringing from Filip's pocket. He took out his mobile, shook his head and whined, 'It does everything,' he said. 'Radio, camera, MP3 player, torch, and it's …'

'Are you afraid?' said Oskar.

Filip held out his hand and let go of the phone. Splash. A faint ringing could be heard as it sank to the bottom.

'Waterproof.'

They paddled in silence. No one complained about blisters or tiredness. Every so often Pi looked through the binoculars. The only thing she saw was Bengt and Bertil bringing up their nets.

They carried on with their journey long after the sun had gone down and the air had turned blue and cool. Mik noticed it was getting easier, that the raft was keeping a good pace. The water had a current.

'We'll stop here,' said Pi. 'The way out is down there, and we've got to tackle the Älg rapids in daylight.'

They tied the raft to some large trees and camouflaged it with leafy branches which they pushed between the logs and spread over the tent. It was impossible to detect, a floating bush.

They crawled into the tent and down into their sleeping-bags.

Mik couldn't sleep. The others were asleep already. Oskar had taken Filip's pillow and Pi was snoring quietly. Mik stared up at the tent roof where mosquitoes and midges were bumping against the canvas. He was listening. The water lapped against the sides of the raft. Occasionally the tent canvas rustled. Far off in the distance was a faint rushing sound. There was a flapping of powerful wings.

The Paragraph flew over mountains, forests and lakes. A demon with talons, sharp teeth and bloody ears. The Paragraph saw everything, heard everything and wanted to know everything. The Paragraph crept in the forest, sniffed along the shore, flew across every sky. Searched for him and would take him. No one could hide from the Paragraph, for he was everywhere.

Mik shook Pi.

'Can you hear that rushing sound?'

'Yes. It's only the noise from the Älg rapids. Go to sleep now.'

Mik crept closer to Pi. She turned on her side and blew warm air into his ear.

~~~

They paddled in silence. It was easy now. The current was getting stronger and stronger. Patches of turbulence and ripples could be seen on the smooth surface. The raft's crew concentrated, heavy lumps growing in their chests. The rushing noise from the Älg rapids got louder. They saw the edge ahead and the spray that rose up from the forest. Faster and faster the raft travelled towards the world's end, where everything tips down into the unknown. The rushing grew to a roar. Now there was no time for regrets. They stopped paddling.

'Oh no,' said Oskar.

Pi looked at Mik.

'Hold on. You mustn't fall off. Promise.'

Mik lay down and held on to some rope. The raft slid over

the threshold and the whole of the Älg rapids lay before them. Wild and roaring. Waves hurled high into the air. Their stomachs sank. The current shook and tugged at the raft and the logs creaked and groaned. Whirling white foamy water. Faster and faster. They spun round and thrashed about. They were riding a monster at full gallop. The waves crashed over them. Oskar lost his paddle. Backpacks and bags were swept overboard. The rapids played with the big, heavy raft as if it were made of bark.

Wave after wave washed over them. The tent was torn down; tent poles snapped. Mik shut his eyes and clung on desperately. The river tugged and tore at his clothes, grabbed hold of his body, wanted to pull him off, drag him down into the whirlpools. Take him. Kill him. Drown him.

Then everything went calm.

Mik looked up. It was over. Perhaps he'd wet himself, but his clothes were soaked through so it didn't matter. They had come down into a kind of small lake. The raft rotated slowly and then followed the river round the curve.

The crew was shaken but unharmed. Oskar and Filip suddenly became quite wild, laughing and shrieking and dancing on the raft.

'Wow!'

'We did it! We're the best.'

Pi looked at Mik and smiled. Water was running from her hair and down over her face. Mik started to laugh too and thumped his chest. It was a long time since he had felt giddy

241

with happiness like this. They were all filled with a bubbling joy. It sparkled like a fizzy drink in their veins. Life itself seemed to start over again. Oskar and Filip couldn't stop leaping around. If you survived the Älg rapids, you could survive anything.

'Woohoo,' shouted Filip. 'Rapids – bring 'em on!'

The raft sailed on down the river. They paddled and steered, using poles to guide them. Pi examined the damage and checked what had been lost in the rapids. Oskar's paddle had gone, but that didn't matter much now because the river carried them forwards. It would be easy to mend the raft and the tent. The logs could be tied together again and they could find more tent poles in the forest. But what about the supplies?

'The food,' said Pi. 'We lost everything except a tin of meatballs and a tin of peas. The matches survived, at least.'

'What are we going to do?' said Oskar. 'We'll starve.'

'No, there will be lots of fish,' said Pi. 'We'll have to do some fishing.'

'I hate fish,' said Oskar.

The sleeping-bags and pillows were soaked through. They hung everything from the mast to dry.

They sailed through deep ravines between vertical rock faces where the air was cool and the sky was a thin blue line above their heads. They worked their way around large rocks between murmuring dark forests. Several times the raft wedged itself against rocks and they had to jump off and pull it free. They came out into wide, open water and had to paddle hard again.

Despite blisters and aching muscles, no one complained. They were on the run; they were on an adventure, and no one could stop them.

Towards evening the current became more powerful. They could hear the low rushing sound of the Borg rapids in the distance and they longed for it with a mixture of terror and delight.

Tired and with their stomachs groaning from hunger, they paddled ashore and secured the raft. Pi divided up the tasks. Oskar and Filip had to repair and strengthen the raft before the next day's journey down the Borg rapids, and the tent needed new poles. She and Mik were going to fish for their dinner.

'I don't eat fish,' said Oskar and started tying together logs that had worked loose.

'Well you'll just have to eat pine cones then,' said Pi, handing Mik a fishing rod.

They walked downstream a short distance and Pi pointed at the flowing water, showing him the good fishing places. He would be fishing in still pools behind big rocks at the edge of the current. That was where the fish were.

Mik kept slipping on the stony bank, got his line tangled up and lost his hook.

Pi caught yellow-speckled trout and grayling with large violet fins on their backs. She laughed at Mik and gave him another line and hook, which soon got stuck high up in a pine tree. He pulled and a pine cone fell down.

'You're just unlucky,' said Pi.

They gutted the fish together. She was good at that, too. Mik thought the insides of the fish were slimy and he found it difficult to cut a straight line across the stomach. Pi showed him how to hold the fish and then it went better.

Oskar and Filip had repaired the raft and the tent looked good, its canvas stretched tightly. They had also gathered sticks and made a fire in a neat hearth.

'Fish is revolting,' said Oskar,

'Mik actually caught a pine cone,' said Pi.

Night fell over the forest. The river gurgled, the fire crackled and the fish grilled on sticks propped up against the flames. They hissed and bubbled. The fat fell in drops. The smell was wonderful.

Mik was wild with hunger. He didn't care if the whole world disintegrated, as long as he could eat first. Pi took a fish from the fire and tasted it. She nodded and Filip and Mik threw themselves forward and took a fish each. They ate with their fingers, cramming the food into their mouths. Oskar pulled a disgusted face.

'Lovely,' said Mik. 'Even the skin.'

He looked across the fire into Pi's eyes. The flames glittered and crackled. She was all right. How all right? Probably an eleven on a scale of one to ten. Maybe even a twelve – hard to tell when she was off the scale.

They chatted round the fire about what would happen after the Borg rapids. But nobody knew. After the Borg rapids they were in unknown territory. Perhaps there were more rapids. Maybe waterfalls. Or perhaps the worst was over and it would be plain sailing to the sea. And then what? Nobody could answer that. They would have to decide then.

Mik put more sticks on the fire and moved the lumps of wood around with a stick. There was something lying there among the glowing embers. Something strange and round. A metal object? He poked it with the stick. A red-hot tin can with bulging sides. And then it exploded. BOOM. Boiling hot meatballs flew in all directions. One hit Oskar right in the middle of his forehead. The fire went out. There were only small embers dotted around the outside.

'What the bloody hell happened?' said Filip.

Oskar held his forehead.

'I put the can in to heat up …'

'Then you probably should have opened it first,' said Mik.

They collected some wood and the fire was soon burning again. Pi was angry.

'Brilliant, Oskar. Now we've only got the peas left.'

Oskar didn't answer. He was walking along the beach and around the forest searching for meatballs. He found a few and that cheered him up.

~~~

Mik woke with a start and sat up. The tent canvas was damp with dew and it was still night. His body was covered in sweat. He had been chased awake by a nightmare. A monster with a dreadful shriek that made the bones in his body shatter like glass. Only a dream, only a dream. He felt himself getting calmer. His heart was racing at top speed. He breathed deeply and lay down again.

Then a shriek came from the forest, right up close. A long-drawn-out shriek. Mik got goosebumps all over his arms, stomach, back and legs. The hairs on the back of his head stood on end. The shriek came again, like an icicle plunged deep into his heart.

He elbowed Pi, who muttered, 'What is it? I want to sleep.'

'Something's shrieking out there. There's something in the forest.'

'There are lots of things in the forest,' said Pi and snuggled down in her sleeping-bag, hugging her pillow.

The shriek came again. Pi opened her eyes wide into two circles and looked at Mik. A heavy beat of wings could be heard over the tent, disappearing down the river.

'Only a bird,' said Pi, and she turned over, punching her pillow.

'A big bird?' said Mik.

'Yes,' said Pi. 'Only a big bird. A bird of prey.'

'Sure?'

'Yes,' she said, sounding irritated. 'Go to sleep now.'

How big? he wanted to ask. But he kept quiet and lay awake until the sun burned through the tent canvas.

246

THE KARMA SNAKE

The roar from the Borg rapids increased, getting louder and louder. They secured everything that was loose onboard.

Pi was in command and gave orders, holding on to the mast. She promised that everything would be all right, that they would manage it. Jaws were clenched, muscles tensed.

They went over the edge and the wild, foaming water took a hard grip of the raft. It whirled and lurched, tumbled and spun. Pi shouted but nobody heard what she said. Ropes snapped, one by one. The shore and the forest rushed past. They held on, battling to stay in place in the middle of a storm of boiling water.

The tent was ripped loose and was swept away. The loosened logs squealed and fought against each other. Mik got his hand trapped and he was almost washed overboard.

Water forced its way into their ears and mouths; it grasped and tore at their bodies. The mast broke in two and Pi was left hanging onto a rope. The raft rose up against a giant rock, rotated and went spinning off into calmer water.

No one was missing, but they exchanged terrified looks. Oskar got sick. Everything had been swept off the raft: mast, tent, sleeping-bags, pillows. Nothing remained. Logs had been wrenched apart and bobbed up and down on their own.

No one cheered. The whole adventure had been swept away. The matches were wet. By some kind of miracle the tin of peas had survived, only the label had been washed off.

'Can we go home now?' said Oskar. 'Have we finished running away?'

Nobody answered. Everyone knew it was a very long way home. Tens of kilometres through forests with no roads.

They dragged the raft ashore and began joining ropes and lashing logs together. They found two paddles tumbling around in a backwater below the rapids, but none of the other equipment. The raft was unstable. They needed more rope.

'But it didn't break up,' said Pi. 'I told you the raft would make it. Didn't I? I was right.'

No one answered.

The river remained calm for the rest of the day. They paddled and used poles to get along. A chilly wind blew up through the valley and the sun hid behind clouds. Their clothes would not dry. Hunger clawed at their stomachs.

They made a camp for the night under a fir tree and made a bed of branches and moss, propping branches all around to make it a proper little hut. Mik thought he heard something carried on the wind: a faint grinding sound, like the noise of a big factory. He didn't mention it. They crawled in under the fir tree and shared the tin of peas.

'I'm sure we'll reach some bridge or village tomorrow,' said Pi. 'We can ring from there and they can come and collect us.'

They crept close together to keep warm. Pi put her arm around Mik.

'The peas weren't exactly filling,' said Filip.

'Eat a pine cone,' said Pi.

Mik hoped they wouldn't come to a bridge or village tomorrow. He hoped … well, what did he hope? To live under a tree with Pi for the rest of his life? If Mik had to choose between going down the rapids again or returning to the Tormentors, he would choose the rapids. But that was his choice. Mik was pretty sure Pi, Oskar and Filip were regretting everything. They could simply have waved him goodbye as he stepped into Parrot Earrings' car. That would have been the easiest thing for them to do. But no, instead they had put the escape plan into action. He liked them very much.

The Paragraph shrieked in the forest and it started to rain.

Pi gathered sorrel and fresh green pine needles for breakfast. They tasted bitter and very green. Like eating the actual forest.

Oskar said, 'I don't want to eat stuff from the flipping forest.'

He spat and coughed and started talking about toast and marmalade. Pi told him to stop, but Oskar laid a breakfast table in thin air.

'Then I'll have one with liver pâté. No I won't, I'll –'

'Shut it,' said Filip, twisting a twig of new pine needles between his fingers.

'Cheese roll,' said Oskar. 'Dipped in hot chocolate so the cheese gets melted and stringy.'

Filip threw the twig right in Oskar's eye and they were soon wrestling among the moss and pine needles.

'This is crap,' shouted Filip. 'We're lost without food and you talk about cheese rolls. I'll murder you.'

Pi separated them.

'We're following the river. We're not lost.'

'And where does that take us, then?' yelled Filip. 'To the sea? To China? I want to go home.'

'Cheese roll,' said Oskar.

Their stomachs cried out. An ocean of corroding digestive juices with only a few pine needles sailing around. Mik said nothing; he thought it was all his fault. He was the one who was the problem. The problem child. Without him they wouldn't be here with only pine needles to eat.

'Liver pâté,' said Oskar, and Filip flew at him again.

'Cheese roll,' shouted Oskar, as Filip stuffed a handful of moss into his mouth.

'Stop!' roared Pi. 'Look at Mik, he's not moaning.'

Filip and Oskar stopped fighting and stared at Mik with sulky expressions which could not be misinterpreted.

Mik pointed at the raft and said, 'We'll get to a bridge or village today, I'm sure.'

'Aaaarrrrgggggghhhh!' bellowed Filip. 'It's all your fault. Do you know that? You're the one with the problem. You're a wino's kid. I haven't got any problems. What the hell am I doing here?'

It went quiet. Mik looked out over the river. Pi tried to untangle her hair. The game had ended long ago.

'Yes,' said Mik. 'I'm a wino's kid. I haven't forgotten that.'

Filip was right. Mik knew this running away was pointless. Every running away was pointless. Even if he took himself ten thousand kilometres away it wouldn't help. Just like Filip said, he was the one with the problem. And you couldn't escape from yourself. You always ended up on a cannibal beach.

'We'll get going now,' said Pi. 'And no talk of food. Otherwise we'll go mad.'

They untied the raft and propelled it out into the river. The sky cleared and the current glittered in the morning sun.

They poled and paddled. They all thought about food. Mik tried thinking about dog poo and porridge, but he would even be able to eat porridge if he only had some jam to go with it. That's how hungry he was.

The river flowed into a deep crevasse in the rock. Dizzying vertical walls of stone rose up on each side. The raft floated on as if in a corridor. The air turned cool and the sun could not penetrate down between the stone walls. The water ran deep and black.

Mik heard the factory sound, dark, heavy and grinding. The raft picked up speed. There was no river bank, only rock straight down into the black water. It didn't sound like water going over rapids. This was something else. Something much worse.

'Pizza,' said Oskar, and Filip went completely crazy. They started to fight, using the paddles, chasing each other round, yelling and waving the oars.

'Shush,' said Pi.

But they kept going.

'Stop it now. Listen.'

Oskar and Filip froze with their paddles in mid air. Something was getting closer. That was how it felt, not that they were on their way towards something. The sound got louder. They couldn't see where it was coming from, the river curved slightly in its gulley. Something immense was approaching.

Everyone looked at Pi and waited for her to say something, hoped that, as usual, she would know what they ought to do.

The raft bumped into the rock wall and spun round. The noise grew and rebounded between the walls. An enormous monster was hunting them, faster and faster. They paddled to one side and tried to hold on to outcrops of rock, but the pull was already too strong. The heavy raft was going too fast and there was no bank to escape to. Only bare flat rock walls. There was no way to make it stop. The raft went round the curve and they saw the river disappear into a huge, steaming, roaring hole.

This was not rapids. This was a waterfall.

Oskar wanted to jump into the water, but Pi stopped him.

'Lie down!' she shouted. 'Lie down and hold on.'

'The Karma Falls!' shouted Mik. 'We're going to die.'

'Mummy!' shouted Oskar.

Filip said nothing. He was one big, gaping mouth. They all lay down and grabbed the rope. Pi reached out her hand to Mik. He took it and squeezed it hard.

The raft went over the edge, standing up on end. The waterfall swallowed them like a serpent shaking its head towards the sky to swallow its prey. The raft fell and landed on stones. Ropes snapped and logs flew in all directions. Mik saw Oskar flying through the air and then he himself was spun round in circles and lost hold of Pi's hand.

He was tossed about among logs and rope, grazed his knees and arms, and was hurled backwards and forwards among bubbles and foam. He was sucked down into deep water and whirled around with logs as if he was in a blender, and felt a ringing blow on his head. Using his legs, he pushed up from the river bed, shooting himself to the surface through the whirls of the current. Swam and fought towards the surface, managed to gulp in some air before being pulled down again.

Mik didn't know which way was up. Perhaps he was swimming towards the bottom. The whale sang in his ear. Whales and snakes and the sky far above. Bubbling, hissing and howling filled his ears. Someone yelled, 'Swim!'

'Swim!'

He saw the sky, gasped some air, and far away stood Pi on a flat piece of rock below the wall of stone.

'Mik!' she screamed. 'Swim. Keep on swimming.'

Filip and Oskar dragged themselves to safety. Mik was sucked down again, rolled over and over and fought with the Snake. He felt it wrap itself round his arms and legs, wind itself around his body. Squeezing.

'You're swimming,' shouted Pi.

The Snake got weaker and weaker. Mik came out of the current and worked his way towards Pi. His muscles burned.

'You can swim.'

Mik lost concentration completely and began to struggle and splash. He sank. Struggled even more and sank faster. Pi jumped in and dragged him up onto the rock.

'You swam,' said Pi.

'Yes,' said Mik. He was absolutely finished, his body shaking. 'I must have done.'

He looked over towards the rushing water, saw the turbulence that rotated under the waterfall. The raft's logs whirled round without getting anywhere.

'Your forehead's bleeding,' said Pi.

Mik felt it with his hand; it turned red.

'It's nothing.'

Things were worse for Oskar. He sat in silence on the flat rock and stared vacantly. They waved their hands in front of his face, shouted in his ears. But no reaction. He was completely gone. His gaze was a thousand kilometres away.

'Oskar has seen the Snake,' said Mik.

'What lousy snake?' yelled Filip. 'There's no snake here. No raft either. No food, nothing. This is so stupid that …'

He started to cry.

'We'll go home now,' said Pi. 'We'll climb up and go home.'

She looked at Mik with eyes that were waiting for his answer.

He nodded.

AUTUMN

The police, the army and local people had been looking for them. A helicopter had searched along the river, but no one could believe they had taken themselves so far in such a short time on a simple raft. They had been looking in the wrong places.

The joy was overwhelming when they returned, dirty and hungry but alive. Parrot Earrings had left long before. Mik was going to be allowed to stay all through the autumn. Lena had fought hard and arranged for him to stay with her until the future placement was decided.

Everyone was happy and Bengt had gone round the whole village with a petition. The Citizens of Selet in Support of Mik Continuing to Live in the Community. All 163 residents of the village had signed their names. The senile and the small babies – all had made their mark on the list. Bengt even went to Bertil's house and, without either of them saying a word to each other, Bertil had added his name.

Bengt said Mik, Pi, Oskar and Filip were the first to have survived a trip over the Stor Falls. It gave them a kind of glory. But Oskar could remember nothing about the raft journey and it was a week before he started talking again. He had been to the hospital in Umeå and had his head X-rayed.

They saw nothing in particular.

'Of course they didn't see anything,' said Filip. 'It's empty in there.'

~~~

As the leaves turned yellow Pi and Mik often went down to the river to fish. It was Mik who wanted to do that. He liked the flowing water, liked the bubbling and rushing. Pi taught him to read the current, to see by the whirls and calm places on the water where rocks and deep places were. For someone with a trained eye the current revealed what the river bed looked like and where the fish were. Mik became a better and better fisherman.

They gutted their catch and grilled it on the beach, sat in the evenings by the campfire and chatted and dreamed as twilight fell and the stars came out. Next year they would build a new raft, bigger and sturdier. One strong enough to reach the sea. They ate fish and fed the fire with logs. The sparks shot up into the sky. They both knew they would never go over the falls again. That was something a person did only once, and according to Bengt it couldn't actually be done at all. They had done something impossible, and you only needed to do that once.

Pi looked at him through the flames.

'Can I try something?'

'Yes. What?'

She came round to his side of the fire. Leaned against his shoulder. He felt her warm breath in his ear. Pi sucked his earlobe; it tickled and he started to laugh. It was … nice.

'I knew it.'

'Knew what?'

'You didn't faint. Your breathing's perfectly calm.'

'Yes,' said Mik.

He didn't feel anything in his chest – no pressure, no cramp. Only his heart beating nice and regularly.

'You've grown,' said Pi, leaning back, taking him in. 'You're almost as tall as Filip. When did that happen?'

'I dunno. I haven't noticed anything.'

She stayed by his side and leaned her head on his shoulder. They stared into the fire. A breeze took hold of the trees. The flames flickered and yellow birch leaves fluttered down around them.

'It's autumn now. And autumn's short up here.'

They walked home through the forest.

'How short?' said Mik.

'Too short,' said Pi.

In the darkness they held hands.

~~~

Mik threw his fishing bag onto the hall floor. There was a pair of shoes he didn't recognise. Trainers, brand new and white. Adult-sized.

'Hello, are you home?' called Lena from the kitchen. 'Someone's come to see you.'

Tony was sitting on the kitchen sofa, drinking coffee.

Tony? Here? Now?

His hair was cut short and he had a downy moustache. Thoughts and feelings flew around chaotically, collided and crashed into each other. It was unreal. Mik opened his mouth and wanted to tell Tony everything all at once, but he only stood, gaping silently and staring.

'Hi,' said Tony and laughed.

'Moustache?' said Mik.

They sat up until late in the evening, talking. Lena made an apple cake and lit candles all over the kitchen. Mik told Tony everything. Ran around the kitchen showing how he, Pi, Oskar and Filip had survived their raft trip with rapids, starvation and the waterfall. Then the miracle when suddenly he could swim and got himself out of the Karma Snake grip. It wasn't as much fun explaining his time with the Tormentors; he made that short. But he boasted that he was no longer afraid of dogs. Not that he liked them, but he wasn't afraid.

Tony didn't say much. He smiled and laughed at Mik's stories. The funniest parts were when Tengil's men were about to brand the mark of Katla in his backside and he was allowed to keep what he had stolen because he was so hungry. Tony doubled over and roared with laughter. Mik was happy.

'I wrote letters,' said Mik. 'Everything was in the letters. Did you get them?'

'Yes,' said Tony. 'They were good.'

'Why didn't you write?'

Tony sat in silence and drew a finger across his moustache.

'I couldn't. Letters are hard, and … well.'

'How long are you staying?'

'Only over the weekend.'

Tony slept on a mattress on the floor in Mik's attic room. Mik woke several times during the night, astonished that Tony was lying there on the floor. That it wasn't a dream, that it was true. But even if it was true it felt like a dream. Tomorrow he would show him the river.

Bengt lent Tony boots and a fishing line.

'So,' said Bengt. 'You're Mik's big brother. He's talked a lot about you.'

Bengt brought out the petition, The Citizens of Selet in Support of Mik Continuing to Live in the Community.

'Well, you're not technically a resident of Selet, but in your capacity as his brother you are fully entitled to sign.'

Tony signed.

'Nice moustache,' said Bengt. 'A bit sparse, but it'll grow.

The boots fitted, and they walked through the forest to the river. The path twisted and turned and was difficult to see. It was Mik and Pi who had trampled the path – or paths. They rarely went the same way through the forest. It was a confusing system of narrow tracks and it was easy to go the wrong way.

'He's a strange old bloke,' said Tony.

'You should see his brother.'

The water of the river reflected and played with the clear, glowing autumn colours of the trees. Red and yellow against the deep blue of the sky. Tony thought it was beautiful. It was straight out of a fairy tale, he said. Clean and bright.

Not a sound apart from the gentle gurgling of the river. Mik pointed out the current, explained what eddies, still pools and current edges meant. That there were troughs, rocks and logs on the river bed that created surface movement. Tony listened with interest to Mik's fishing tips about finding small fish in the shallows and bigger ones at the current edges in the still pools. He showed his big brother the best places where the fish were sure to bite. Then he went further upstream.

Mik noticed that Tony was quite clumsy, his feet slipping on the stony shore and into the water. And the way he fished was completely wrong, not at all like Mik had shown him. But it didn't matter. He was here and Mik couldn't take his eyes off him. His big brother was here and they were fishing together. Mik had a bite and pulled a big grayling out of the river. He cheered and shouted. Tony turned round and Mik held up the fish.

'Good,' said Tony. 'That's a nice one.'

Mik caught one more and Tony slipped into the water again. He tipped the water out of his boots and said it didn't matter, soon he would be landing a really huge one. The biggest one of all.

Mik thought that if that was the case he would be incredibly lucky, because he was doing everything wrong.

'Cast your line in the pools,' called Mik.

~~~

Leaves fell from the trees and were carried off by the current. They fished until evening. Tony caught some fish, too, but they were small ones. Mik gutted the fish quickly and expertly while Tony stood beside him thinking it seemed a bit messy.

'Smart knife,' he said.

'Bengt gave it to me.'

'You're all right here,' said Tony. 'That makes me happy. For your sake.'

They gathered sticks and made a fire on the shore. Tony emptied the water out of his boots again and hung his socks up to dry. Mik began to barbecue the fish.

'How clever you are,' said Tony.

'It was just luck. You got a few too.'

'Oh, I can't do this kind of thing. But that's not what I meant.'

Mik turned the fish. The fat bubbled and dropped down into the fire. Tony turned his socks, warmed his feet by the fire and went on, 'I mean you've come through this okay. That's what I wanted to see. It makes me happy. Do you understand that, Mik? You make me happy.'

'You've come through it okay too,' said Mik and tasted one of the fish.

'I couldn't write any letters. I tried, but I couldn't do it.'

'It's hard writing letters,' said Mik, handing Tony a fish.

262

In an odd way, Tony felt like a stranger to Mik. Something had changed. It wasn't only the moustache. His way of talking, of moving, was different. Maybe no one except Mik would notice. Maybe something had happened to him too. To his way of seeing and listening. Mik didn't know. Maybe something had happened to the whole world. Maybe it was like the river – familiar eddies and currents float past but never exactly the same, always a little different, always new. Where had Tony been? What had he done? He hadn't actually told Mik anything.

They ate in silence. Dusk fell. A terrifying shriek sounded from the forest. Tony turned hastily around and sat as if frozen to the spot. The shriek came again.

'It's only a bird,' said Mik.

'Blimey.'

'You could live here too,' said Mik.

'That would be difficult,' said Tony.

'Why? You just have to move here. Lena can fix it. She'll fill in a few forms and send them to the Paragraph.'

'The paragraph?'

'Yeah, and then we can go fishing every day, and next summer we can build a –'

'Mik,' said Tony, looking at him over the flames, his eyes shiny with tears. 'It's not that simple.'

Mik was about to say something. He opened his mouth, but Tony held up his hand. The look in his eyes had changed. It was scared and darted about. He gazed into the fire, then out into the darkness across the river. A tear shone on his cheek. He filled his lungs and then exhaled slowly.

'Remember that gun in the wardrobe?'

'Yes, it had gone.'

'Dennis and I, we … we went into a filling station in Huvudsta. We got some money, cigarettes. The place I'm living now … I'll be there some time.'

Mik understood what Tony was saying. He understood the meaning of the words, individually, but his brain refused to put them together. He shot up, ran to the river and started hurling pebbles out into the pitch darkness. Pebble after pebble. Hard and far. He tried to hit something out there in the darkness. Something smack in the head. The hate, smack in the head. He threw until the pain dug and tore at his shoulder. Tony stayed by the fire. An unmoving silhouette, bent forward like an old man. Mik squeezed a pebble hard in his hand.

'What's going on with Dad? Do you know anything?'

'No,' said Tony. 'I don't know anything.'

'He's a zombie,' said Mik and dropped the pebble.

Tony put his socks back on. They had dried. He stepped into the boots and said, 'There's only you and me now.'

'Yeah. Zombie children.'

'And we'll get through this.'

'Yeah,' said Mik. 'Shall we go home now?'

Early on Sunday morning, Lena and Mik went to wave Tony off from the bus stop in the square. Mik started to cry, which made Tony start crying too. Lena tried to comfort them and said she was sure they would see each other again soon, that Tony could come and visit whenever he wanted. That everything was going to be all right.

'It'll all work out,' she said, and then she started crying.

Mik cried all the way home. They walked past the school, over the bridge, past Gustavsson's dog, who stepped aside. Mik saw the world through a grey mist, and it wasn't the same world any more since Tony had been here. Whether it was good or bad he didn't know, but there was just so much he had suddenly remembered that he didn't want to remember. It was just that so many things were the way they were and he didn't want them to be the way they were.

'Look,' said Lena, pointing up at the top of a birch tree down by Bengt's house.

The hawk owl was sitting there.

THE LETTER

The last remaining leaves fell from the trees. The days became shorter, the nights longer and colder. Thin, clear ice settled along Lake Selet's shoreline. Lena began burning books again to keep the electricity bills down.

One Tuesday the first snow fell. It fell heavily. The whole world turned white as if someone had waved a magic wand. All the schoolchildren ran out at break time and started throwing snowballs, sliding on their backsides and rubbing snow in the faces of those who deserved it. They cheered, laughed and shouted.

Synchro-Bertil had forecast from perch fins that it would be a cold winter to break all records. Long, plenty of snow and very cold. It seemed as if he was right. The temperature plunged. Clear, starry nights came with the flashing northern lights, and steam rose from the lake.

Mik lay awake and heard the song the ice made as it was forming. Long, magical notes the cold played as the water changed and set solid. The moon was suspended up there and the hawk owl sat in the tree. Everything was white. The fir trees in the forest on the mountainside stood weighed down with snow just like in a winter fairy tale, and smoke rose from every chimney in the village. The ice land was back.

Mik sat on the sledge with the headwind piercing his face like ice-cold needles. Bengt kept a fast pace. The ice on Lake Selet lay shiny, free of snow and untouched, like glass. Mik had to shout to make Bengt hear him.

'How can you tell there's going to be lots of winter by looking at perch?'

'You can't.'

'Yes, Synchro-Bertil can.'

'The only thing Bertil can do is talk a load of rubbish.'

'There's lots of winter now,' said Mik.

'Winter is winter,' said Bengt, and that was the end of the conversation about Bertil's perch.

They stopped at the first hole. Bengt used his axe to break through the ice that had formed overnight, and Mik grabbed the fishing line.

'We've got one. He's big.'

His arms twitched and jerked. The line hissed round in the hole.

'It's an ice dragon,' said Mik and slipped and fell over.

Bengt laughed.

'Take it easy now. Haul it up.'

Mik struggled and an enormous gaping mouth came up out of the hole and chewed at thin air with its fangs. Its jaws slammed shut with a dull thud. Bengt crouched down and took a strong hold around its gills.

'Watch out for the slime!' shouted Mik. 'You can be paralysed. They spit out slime and you can go blind, lame or deaf.'

'We'll be making fishballs out of this one,' said Bengt. 'They're good, just like meatballs.'

'Isn't it going to France?'

'No, Konsum Lasse has finished with all that. He's got rid of the pike business too.'

Bengt laid the fish in the box, then suddenly looked up.

They heard the roar of an engine going at top speed and a sledge came travelling at a terrifying pace over the ice. It was Synchro-Bertil.

'Has he got an engine on his sledge?' said Mik.

'Yes, dammit. The idiot has attached the chainsaw, with its blade down in the ice.

'Why don't you sell your fish to ICA too?'

'No,' said Bengt. 'Here you're either a Konsum person or an ICA person.'

'That's what Lena said, but she does her shopping at ICA now.'

'I wouldn't set foot in the place.'

'Where do you do your shopping?'

'Gustavsson does it for me.'

'At ICA?'

'Yes.'

Synchro-Bertil roared past, ice flying up from the chainsaw blade.

'Hope he drives right through the ice,' said Bengt. 'Right through, with sledge and chainsaw and the whole shebang.'

'So you can save him?'

'Yep, so I can save him.'

～～～

Mik stamped the snow from his boots on the front steps, walked inside and hung his mittens on the heater. He opened his mouth to say something about the ice-dragon balls that Bengt was going to make.

Lena looked as if she had gone totally mad.

She shouted, 'I'm not good enough. Those bastards insist I'm not good enough.'

She waved an envelope around, slung it down on the table and threw her arms out wide.

'I hate them,' she shouted. 'Do you understand, Mik? Hate them.'

He understood. It started somewhere down at his feet like a paralysis, wandered up through his legs and into his body, in towards the heart. Lena looked at him and clenched her fists.

'Why aren't I good enough?'

She picked up the vase from the table, the one that had held the water lily in the summer, and threw it straight at the wall. Mik's drawing of the hawk owl fluttered away and the photo of her dead dog fell to the floor. The vase didn't break. Lena cried out, picked it up and threw it at the iron stove.

This time it broke.

RED ROSES

Their teacher had pulled down a large map from the ceiling like a roller blind. They were doing geography and studying rivers and mountain ranges. The pupils sat in twos with their school atlases in front of them, looking for the Urals, The Apennines, the Elbe and the Oder, the Caucasus, Carpathians and the Pyrenees.

Mik and Pi were working together. They had been given a blank map and were putting the right name in the right place. The rivers had to be coloured blue and the mountain ranges brown. Mik coloured in and Pi spelt out the awkward names.

'The police,' said Filip.

All work stopped. Mik looked out through the window. A police car was parked in the school playground along with a normal silver-coloured car. Their doors were wide open. Their engines were running and the exhaust fumes formed clouds in the cold. But the cars were empty. How mysterious! A police car from Umeå? There hadn't been one of those in the village since Bertil had been taken in for illegal hunting.

Mik realised what was going on, and then Parrot Earrings and Gold Tooth entered the classroom, followed by two policemen. The teacher was frightened at first, then angry.

They were storming the school as if they were arresting a bank robber. She swore at them. 'And what the hell is this supposed to mean?'

Parrot Earrings was out of breath.

'We're here to take someone into care, according to the law.'

'Police?'

'We have reason to expect trouble,' said Gold Tooth.

'Trouble?' said the teacher. 'This isn't how you do things. You can't come bursting in here, into my classroom, for goodness' sake.'

'A decision has been made about a care order,' said Parrot Earrings.

'I don't care about that,' said the teacher. 'We are having a lesson and don't want to be disturbed. And does Lena know about this?'

'It won't take long,' said Gold Tooth. He nodded towards the policemen and pointed to where Mik was sitting. The policemen exchanged glances, looked down at their boots and puffed out their cheeks.

'Fetch him and put him in the car,' said Parrot Earrings. 'We're in a hurry. We must make sure this doesn't all go wrong.'

'It already has,' said the teacher. 'No one here is going to be fetched. In this school I make the decisions.'

She prodded the stomach of one of the policemen. He was tall and sturdy. She had to lean her head backwards to be able to look him in the eye.

'You're called Roland, I think?'

'Yes, I am.'

'You're Erik Pål's boy, aren't you? From Fällfors?'

'Yes.'

'I taught you from first grade up to third grade in Fällfors School. Do you remember? Roland who couldn't say his Rs. Loland.'

The policeman's face turned red and the class went silent, everyone holding their breath. A big, grown-up policeman was changed to Loland who couldn't say his Rs. He probably wished he had come to take away an armed robber, not a boy on behalf of the social services.

'And you always had a runny nose,' said their teacher, 'and carried about one of those soft dolls. But now you have a gun.'

The other policeman laughed.

'How's your father these days?' the teacher asked.

'He's in sheltered accommodation. A bit forgetful, but otherwise fairly well.'

Parrot Earrings and Gold Tooth realised that their speedy and smooth collection was not going to happen. This was going to be awkward. The pupils stared wide-eyed at the policeman who was called Loland and had played with dolls.

'Can you say your Rs now?' asked Filip.

'I certainly can. Red roses, row, round, rhubarb.'

'Rhubarb?' said the other policeman.

Time seemed to stand still and vibrate. One second. Two

seconds. Three seconds. As if the cogs in the clock mechanism were slipping.

The class broke out in hysterical laughter. Mik made a leap past the social workers and the policemen. Out of the classroom, out of the school.

Gold Tooth chased after him and caught him up in the playground. He grabbed hold of Mik's arm and held it so tight it hurt and wrestled him towards the car. Mik kicked, screamed and bit. Wriggled out of his jumper, out of the clutches of Gold Tooth, picked up a hockey stick from the ground and started waving it around in front of him. Was backed into a corner between the brick wall and the fence beside the river.

The whole class, the teacher, the policemen and Parrot Earrings came out from the school. The smaller pupils were frightened and started to cry. The policemen stood still. They were not sure what to do. Pi threw an ice ball at Gold Tooth's neck. Filip and several others copied her. Parrot Earrings became confused.

Mik lashed out with the hockey stick. Again and again and again. Gold Tooth leaped out of the way.

'You're not taking me,' said Mik. 'I'm staying here.'

'That's not for you to decide.'

'Oh, yes, it is,' said Mik.

He was afraid and cried through clenched teeth. The tears felt cold as they trickled down his cheeks. They wouldn't take him. Not alive.

'Give me the stick now, and we'll do this nice and calmly.'

Mik shot forwards and struck a blow right on Gold Tooth's knees. Gold Tooth bent over and collapsed in the snow, swearing. Mik ran out onto the road and across the bridge. Gold Tooth got up onto his feet and raced quickly after him, gaining on him, but on the other side of the bridge Gustavsson's dog launched himself at him.

Mik got away; he knew where he was going, and no one could follow him there. Not even the Paragraph. He ran down to the lake and out onto the ice.

A SWORD OF ICE

A black, round hole. Shiny ice and an eye in the middle of Lake Selet. He slithered carefully to the edge. It could just as easily have been the end of the world. Or a black hole in the universe with an endless magnetic pull. The surface swayed.

Bengt came by on his sledge, on the way home from his pike fishing.

'Mik, what the hell are you doing out there? Get away from that ice hole.'

'No. They're here.'

A group of people staggered out onto the ice. It was Mik's class. And their teacher. And two policemen. And then Parrot Earrings and Gold Tooth. Bengt understood the situation very clearly. The policemen came first.

'Stop' yelled Bengt. 'The ice is very thin.'

He got them to stop at a safe distance and explained how treacherous the ice was.

'And out there, where the boy's standing, the ice is only a few centimetres thick.'

Confusion followed and the situation became deadlocked. Nobody knew what they ought to do. They called to Mik, but he didn't answer.

Lena came out onto the ice. She was distressed and angry and had a good mind to strangle Parrot Earrings. They looked at each other and then Parrot Earrings turned her head away. Mik's classmates pointed and people talked on their mobiles. The fire service was on its way, and a helicopter too, they were saying. Pi started to cry.

Lena took hold of Bengt's arm.

'What do you think?'

'Well, no one can get out there. The ice won't hold them.'

'What shall we do?'

'Nothing,' said Bengt, and he looked at Lena.

She saw the flash of a smile on his face. 'He's not stupid. This will give them time to think a little. To freeze and think. That's good.'

Now Parrot Earrings and Gold Tooth were talking with the policemen. Bengt looked at them out of the corner of his eye and saw the policemen shaking their heads.

'You're Erik Pål's boy, aren't you?' called Bengt.

'Yes.'

'A good man, he is,' said Bengt.

'What shall we do?' asked the policeman.

'Nothing,' said Bengt, and, turning towards Mik, he made a funnel with his fingers and shouted, 'Have you got the knife?'

Mik slapped his side, where his belt was.

'Good.'

Bengt took a sighting on Mik against the mast on

Granberget. Travelled a bit to the left and took a sighting again from the church tower towards Tallåsen and then further on towards the southern end of the lake. Looked back and calculated again, taking a new sighting towards the boathouse. Then he tested the stretch to the south, down the lake. At full speed with his kick sledge. Twice. It was actually quite strange to look at.

He breathed heavily and muttered breathlessly, 'It might be all right. But that current's bloody strong.'

'What do you mean?' said Lena.

'In case. There's good visibility through the ice. Shiny, clear and good all the way from the ice hole and down the lake.'

'In case?' said Lena.

'Yes, in case.'

Parrot Earrings was nervous and tugged at the policemen.

'You're really going to have to do something now.'

'Such as what?'

Bengt glided up to them on his kick sledge and said quietly, 'It'll be your fault if he falls through. Just so you know. Everyone here knows that.'

He pulled a crumpled piece of paper from his pocket and handed it to Parrot Earrings.

'Here. A petition. The whole village has signed it. Even Gustavsson: 163 residents.'

'But the decision is –'

'Obviously you don't understand,' said Bengt. 'It's a

strong current. If he falls in he'll go under the ice and if we're lucky we'll find his body in the autumn. That's if the river doesn't sweep him out to sea. Then we'll never find him.'

'But …' attempted Parrot Earrings. 'But we –'

Bengt interrupted her. 'It's impossible to be closer to death than he is now. But you don't seem to get it. Go back to Stockholm! You're murdering him. Bloody child murderers. I'll –'

Bengt grabbed his axe from the pike box. Lena dragged him away from Parrot Earrings. Bengt swore and muttered about authorities and bureaucrats but then calmed down, put away the axe and looked silently across the ice at Mik.

Mik saw all the people. There was a cold wind and he was only wearing a thin jumper. His knees shook. His jaw quivered. How stupid not to have grabbed his jacket. But even if he had been standing here in only his underpants, he wouldn't have left the ice hole.

More and more people gathered. The whole village, perhaps. He couldn't hear what they were saying. Someone slipped over. The ice creaked.

Lena held her jacket closed tight against the wind. An hour had passed without anything happening. Should this kind of thing really be allowed to happen?

'Why aren't I good enough?' she said out loud to the wind. 'He's been fine here. He's been cared for. Ask anyone. He's been fine here. I've been fine too. Should it really be allowed to happen like this? All you need to do is say he can stay.'

The policeman who was called Roland made it clear that they were not going to help with the care order, that it felt very uncomfortable and that they were probably going to have to report this, however it turned out. A child should not be treated like this.

'It's possible you do this kind of thing in Stockholm, but up here we don't chase children out onto thin ice. You're going to have to resolve this now.'

More people walked onto the ice. These people were unfamiliar. One had a camera and was a photographer. The other was a journalist. Someone had phoned the local newspaper. A fire engine with its flashing blue light pulled up on the road. The firemen untied a small dinghy that they had on a trailer and pulled it out onto the ice. They spoke to the policemen and to the teacher.

Mik saw that something was happening. Changing. His teacher gathered together all the pupils and took them back on land. But Pi remained, standing next to Lena.

The journalist spoke with Parrot Earrings and then with Lena and Bengt. The photographer took pictures. Was that good or bad? The firemen shook their heads. Two of them began to struggle into their wetsuits and air cylinders up by the fire engine.

Bengt broke away from the group and travelled towards him, slowly and cautiously. He stopped some distance away. The ice swayed and there were dull cracking sounds.

'Are you cold?'

'Yes.'

'You can come now.'

'Can I stay?'

'Yes.'

'Forever?'

'There's some damned stupid authority that has to look at the situation again. No one can promise anything here and now on the ice.'

Mik did not move from the hole.

'I want to know now.'

'Please, Mik. When it comes to authorities, you can never get a sensible, straightforward answer. To ask these idiots to be able to answer here on the ice is just not possible. But the local paper's here and I've told them what to write. Those Stockholmers will be worth nothing. You're as good as home now. It's all right. The paper's having a go at Parrot Earrings now. She won't have a feather left. They did the same thing to the leader of the council last year, when the paper mill bribed him with a trip to Dubai.'

Mik took a step towards Bengt.

The ice broke. A slight creak and a small, dull explosion.

Mik fell in among clinking ice floes. The cold shot like a frozen sword up through his backbone. A sword of ice. His lungs emptied of air.

'The knife,' shouted Bengt. 'The knife.'

Mik got a hold on the edge of the ice but the current

swept under his legs and dragged at his body. He looked for the knife. Fumbled with no feeling in his fingers. Got the knife out of the sheath and dropped it. He was sucked down, sucked away, glided with his hands against the underside of the ice. Scraped it with his nails. Tried to swim up against the ice but was dragged further and further away.

His body turned numb and was carried gently through the water. He saw all the beautiful patterns in the ice, all the air bubbles which hovered inside. The frozen planets in a wall of dark blue glass. The water wanted him, and now it was going to get him. The whale sang in his ear. Long, mournful notes. The whale in Lake Selet. He saw it. He followed it. Would it show him the way?

Lena cried out and Pi started running towards the ice hole but was held tight by the policemen. Bengt followed Mik's journey under the ice. He could make out the boy's pale hands, which pressed against the underside and glided along with the current.

'Don't drown,' shouted Bengt. Even though he knew Mik couldn't hear. 'You mustn't drown.'

Mik's face shimmered, diffuse as through a frosty pane of glass. Bengt travelled fast over the lake. Cast the sledge from him and hacked a hole in the ice with his axe.

The ice shards whirled. There wasn't much time; never had it been so urgent.

Bengt hacked wildly. Water and ice flew about. He made the hole bigger and at the very last minute made it big enough.

281

Mik felt it getting warmer and warmer. It was lovely, but odd. He had run off without his jacket. It got lighter. He saw the light. Was he there? I can see the light. Where would he get to now? And who was lifting him? Who was struggling with his legs?

Mik came gliding under the ice. Bengt plunged his arms into the water and heaved him out.

Mik coughed and threw up. Bengt took off his overcoat and wrapped it around him.

'Where am I?' said Mik.

'Home.'